SEA MONSTERS

CREDITS

AUTHORS: Miguel Colon, Michael "solomani" Mifsud, Robert J. Grady, Mark Hart, Jeff Ibach, Alex Riggs, Scott D. Young, Jeff Lee, Matt Kimmel, and Jason Nelson

ARTISTS: Simon Aan, Hanyo Arte, Bruno Balixa, Guillermo Cartay, Nicholas Cato, Alex Chystiakov, Frank Hessefort, Michael Jaecks, Jason Juta, Chris Kimball, Tim Kings-Lynne, Matthias Kinnigkeit, Dio Mahesa, Chris McFann, Andrea Montano, Mitch Mueller, Evan Surya Nugraha, Beatrice Pelagatti, Peyeyo, Arrahman Rendi, Julio Rocha, Chris Smith, Bob Storrar, John Tedrick, Jon Tonello, Justin Tumey, Steve Wood

DESIGN AND LAYOUT: Rick Kunz

5E DEVELOPMENT: Miguel Colon, David N. Ross, Michael "solomani" Mifsud, Robert J. Grady, James-Levi Cooke, Ismael Alvarez, Scott D. Young, and Jason Nelson

CHIEF EXECUTIVE OFFICER: Jason Nelson

CHIEF STRATEGIC OFFICER: Shirline Wilson

CHIEF BUSINESS OFFICER: Rachel Ventura

Sea Monsters (5E) © 2021, Legendary Games; Authors Miguel Colon, Michael "solomani" Mifsud, Robert J. Grady, Mark Hart, Jeff Ibach, Alex Riggs, Scott D. Young, Jeff Lee, Matt Kimmel, and Jason Nelson.
ISBN: 978-1-955320-02-3
First printing June 2021.
Printed in China.

Legendary Games
524 SW 321st St.
Federal Way, WA 98023-5656
makeyourgamelegendary.com

Sea Monsters (5E) © 2021, Legendary Games; Authors Michael Ritter, Michael "solomani" Mifsud, Robert J. Grady, Mark Hart, Jeff Ibach, Alex Riggs, Scott D. Young, Jeff Lee, Matt Kimmel, and Jason Nelson.
System Reference Document. © 2000, Wizards of the Coast, Inc.; Authors Jonathan Tweet, Monte Cook, Skip Williams, based on material by E. Gary Gygax and Dave Arneson.
System Reference Document 5.0 Copyright 2016, Wizards of the Coast, Inc.; Authors Mike Mearls, Jeremy Crawford, Chris Perkins, Rodney Thompson, Peter Lee, James Wyatt, Robert J. Schwalb, Bruce R. Cordell, Chris Sims, and Steve Townshend, based on original material by E. Gary Gygax and Dave Arneson.
The Hypertext d20 SRD. © 2004, Jans W Carton.
Alien Bestiary (5E) © 2018, Legendary Games; Lead Designer: Jason Nelson. Authors: Anthony Adam, Kate Baker, John Bennet, Eytan Bernstein, Robert Brookes, Russ Brown, Duan Byrd, Jeff Dahl, Robyn Fields, Joel Flank, Matt Goodall, Robert J. Grady, Jim Groves, Steven T. Helt, Thurston Hillman, Tim Hitchcock, Nick Hite, Daniel Hunt, Mike Kimmel Marshall, Isabelle Lee, Jeff Lee, Lyz Liddell, Jason Nelson, Richard Pett, Tom Phillips, Alistair J. Rigg, Alex Riggs, Wendall Roy, Mike Shel, Neil Spicer, Todd Stewart, Russ Taylor, Rachel Ventura, Mike Welham, George Loki Williams, Scott Young.
Alien Codex (5E) © 2019, Legendary Games; Lead Designer: Jason Nelson. Authors: Anthony Adam, Kate Baker, John Bennet, Eytan Bernstein, Robert Brookes, Russ Brown, Duan Byrd, Paris Crenshaw, Jeff Dahl, Robyn Fields, Joel Flank, Matt Goodall, Robert J. Grady, Jim Groves, Steven T. Helt, Thurston Hillman, Tim Hitchcock, Nick Hite, Daniel Hunt, Mike Kimmel Marshall, Isabelle Lee, Jeff Lee, Lyz Liddell, Jason Nelson, Richard Pett, Tom Phillips, Jeff Provine, Alistair J. Rigg, Alex Riggs, Wendall Roy, Mike Shel, Neil Spicer, Todd Stewart, Russ Taylor, Rachel Ventura, Mike Welham, George Loki Williams, Scott Young.
Pathfinder Roleplaying Game Core Rulebook. © 2009, Paizo Publishing, LLC; Author: Jason Bulmahn, based on material by Jonathan Tweet, Monte Cook, and Skip Williams.
Pathfinder Roleplaying Game Gamemastery Guide. © 2010, Paizo Publishing, LLC; Authors: Cam Banks, Wolfgang Baur, Jason Bulmahn, Jim Butler, Eric Cagle, Graeme Davis, Adam Daigle, Joshua J. Frost, James Jacobs, Kenneth Hite, Steven Kenson, Robin Laws, Tito Leati, Rob McCreary, Hal Maclean, Colin McComb, Jason Nelson, David Noonan, Richard Pett, Rich Redman, Sean K Reynolds, F. Wesley Schneider, Amber Scott, Doug Seacat, Mike Selinker, Lisa Stevens, James L. Sutter, Russ Taylor, Penny Williams, Skip Williams, Teeuwynn Woodruff.
Tome of Beasts. Copyright 2016, Open Design; Authors Chris Harris, Dan Dillon, Rodrigo Garcia Carmona, and Wolfgang Baur.
Tome of Beasts 2. © 2020 Open Design LLC; Authors Wolfgang Baur, Celeste Conowitch, Darrin Drader, James Introcaso, Philip Larwood, Jeff Lee, Kelly Pawlik, Brian Suskind, Mike Welham.
Tome of Horrors © 2018, Frog God Games, LLC; Authors: Kevin Baase, Erica Balsley, John "Pexx" Barnhouse, Christopher Bishop, Casey Christofferson, Jim Collura, Andrea Costantini, Jayson 'Rocky' Gardner, Zach Glazar, Meghan Greene, Scott Greene, Lance Hawvermale, Travis Hawvermale, Ian S. Johnston, Bill Kenower, Patrick Lawinger, Rhiannon Louve, Ian McGarty, Edwin Nagy, James Patterson, Nathan Paul, Patrick N. Pilgrim, Clark Peterson, Anthony Pryor, Greg Ragland, Robert Schwalb, G. Scott Swift, Greg A. Vaughan, and Bill Webb.
Aegis of Empires 3: When Comes the Moon (5E) © 2020, Legendary Games; Authors: Matthew Goodall and Greg A. Vaughan. Adapted by Mark Hart.
Aegis of Empires 5: Race for Shataakh-uLm (5E) © 2020, Legendary Games; Authors: Tom Knauss and Greg A. Vaughan. Adapted by Robert J. Grady and Ismael Alvarez.

TABLE OF CONTENTS

What You Will Find Inside Sea Monsters

Sea Monsters is the latest installment in the *Beasts of Legend* series from Legendary Games, bringing you richly detailed and evocatively described monsters for the 5th Edition of the world's most famous roleplaying game, drawing upon the myths and legends of the real world and throughout the history of RPGs. You can check out the fantastic flair of these monster accessories in the companion volumes *Mythos Monsters, Coldwood Codex, Boreal Bestiary, Construct Codex,* and *Beasts of the East!* The Legendary Games tradition is to combine rich story and background, innovative layout, beautiful aesthetics, and excellence in design that is second to none, allowing you to enliven and enrich your campaign in amazing and exciting ways. This product is the latest in that tradition, and we hope you enjoy using it as much as we enjoyed making it. Game on!

- Jason Nelson

Special Electronic Features

We've hyperlinked this product internally from the Table of Contents and externally with links to the official System Reference Document or 5eSRD. If it is in the core rulebook, we generally didn't link to it unless the rule is an obscure one. The point is not to supersede the game books, but rather to help support you, the player, in accessing the rules, especially those from newer books or that you may not have memorized.

About Legendary Games

Legendary Games is an all star team of authors and designers, founded by Clark Peterson of Necromancer Games, Inc. and managed by Jason Nelson, Legendary Games uses a cooperative, team-based approach to bring you, the Paizo fan, the best expansion material for your game. We are gamers and storytellers first, and we believe that passion shows in our products. So check us out, and Make Your Game Legendary! Visit us on Facebook, follow us on Twitter, and check out our website at www.makeyourgamelegendary.com.

INTRODUCTION

Sea monsters are iconic foes for any fantasy campaign, dating back to the earliest mythologies. Deadly chthonic beasts like Apep and Tiamat were conceived by the Egyptians and Babylonians as water serpents, representing all that lay beneath the swirling, churning waters where all humanity's cleverness could not save them from the water's deadly embrace. From horselords that fear the "poison water" of the oceans to simple riverfolk justly wary of the eddies, whorls, and whirlpools of the great rivers, the water itself always has held the threat of death alongside the promise of life. But out there, in the depths, beneath the surface, just look on any antique map and seek for the words: "Here there be MONSTERS." The idea of unknown, unseen THINGS out there beneath the waves has always fascinated us. Movies are replete with amphibious gargantua from the depths of the sea alongside aquatic abductors both living and undead. We never really know from whence they come, and it is only at the very edge of our capabilities to strike back against them in the briny depths to which they retreat when their hunger for flesh or for captives is sated.

This book brings you over sixty terrifying marine menaces drawn from a variety of sources, from folklore and mythology like bunyips and tritons, or titanic foes like Scylla and Charybdis, as well as real-world creatures like the megalodon, dinichtys, or the great white whale. Not every "sea monster" is truly monstrous; some like the selkie and seaweed leshy could even be friendly and helpful if approached in the right way. Some are simply engines of destruction, like the sea serpent or slaughtermaw lamprey, or by the ancient programming of an advanced antediluvian society like the clockwork leviathan. Some, however, are wholly evil in every respect, like the ghoul-breeding incutilis, the sinister reef hag, or the piratical draugr crews sailing in their ships of the damned. From classic sea monsters of fantasy and fiction to entirely new creatures just for you *Sea Monsters* brings you a ton of terrific terrors from the briny depths below for your 5E campaign!

AQUATIC ADVENTURING

Aquatic terrain is the least hospitable to most PCs, because they can't breathe there. Aquatic terrain doesn't offer the variety that land terrain does. The ocean floor holds many marvels, including undersea analogues of any of the terrain elements described earlier in this section, but if characters find themselves in the water because they were pushed off the deck of a pirate ship, the tall kelp beds hundreds of feet below them don't matter. Accordingly, the only important distinction for dealing with aquatic terrain is generally whether it is flowing water (such as streams and rivers) and non-flowing water (such as lakes and oceans).

The basic rules for aquatic terrain and combat underwater are presented in the **5E System Reference Document** but are presented here in summary for ease of reference.

Swimming: Lakes and oceans simply require a swim speed or successful Strength (Athletics) checks to move through (DC 10 in calm water, DC 15 in rough water, DC 20 in stormy water). Characters need a way to breathe if they're underwater; failing that, they risk drowning. When underwater, characters can move in any direction. Any character can wade in relatively calm water that isn't over his head, no check required. Similarly, swimming in calm water only requires Strength (Athletics) skill checks with a DC of 10. Characters proficient in Athletics can swim easily in calm water without needing to make checks.

A creature without a swimming speed must succeed on a DC 10 Constitution saving throw for each hour it spends swimming or gain one level of exhaustion. If a creature has a swimming speed, it uses the standard travel pace rules in the SRD.

Underwater Combat: When making a melee weapon attack, a creature that doesn't have a swimming speed (either natural or granted by magic) has disadvantage on the attack roll unless the weapon is a dagger, javelin, shortsword, spear, or trident.

A ranged weapon attack automatically misses a target beyond the weapon's normal range. Even against a target within normal range, the attack roll has disadvantage unless the weapon is a crossbow, a net, or a weapon that is thrown like a javelin (including a spear, trident, or dart).

Creatures and objects that are fully immersed in water have resistance to fire damage.

DROWNING

A creature can hold its breath for a number of minutes equal to 1 + its Constitution modifier (minimum of 30 seconds).

When a creature runs out of breath or is choking, it can survive for a number of rounds equal to its Constitution modifier (minimum of 1 round). At the start of its next turn, it drops to 0 hit points and is dying, and it can't regain hit points or be stabilized until it can breathe again.

For example, a creature with a Constitution of 14 can hold its breath for 3 minutes. If it starts suffocating, it has 2 rounds to reach air before it drops to 0 hit points.

STEALTH AND DETECTION UNDERWATER

How far you can see underwater depends on the water's clarity. As a guideline, creatures can see 4d8 × 10 feet if the water is clear, and 1d8 × 10 feet if it's murky. Moving water is always murky, unless it's in a particularly large, slow-moving river.

Invisibility: An invisible creature displaces water and leaves a visible, body-shaped "bubble" where the water was displaced. Being invisible underwater gives a creature advantage on Dexterity (Stealth) checks, but on a failed check, opponents can see the invisible creature's location and size (though not its appearance or specific features). Creatures attacking an invisible creature have disadvantage on their attack rolls.

Falling and Diving into Water: If the water is at least 10 feet deep, the first 20 feet of falling do no damage. A fall of up to 30 feet deals 1d3 bludgeoning damage, while a fall of 40 feet or more deals 1d6 bludgeoning damage, plus 1d6 for every additional 10 feet fallen.

Characters who deliberately dive into water at least 10 feet deep (20 feet deep for fall over 60 feet) can reduce falling damage from a dive, treating the fall as 10 feet shorter with a successful DC 11 Strength (Athletics) or Dexterity (Acrobatics) check, plus an additional 10 feet shorter for every 1 point by which they exceed the DC.

DEEP WATER

Very deep water is generally pitch black, requiring darkvision or other exceptional senses to navigate unless a light source is provided. In addition, in deep water the pressure of the water can impact traveling. A creature traveling at a depth greater than 100 feet but less than 200 feet treats every two hours of travel as if suffering from a forced march as detailed in the **System Reference Document 5.1**. A creature traveling at a depth greater than 200 feet treats every hour of travel as if suffering from a forced march.

The Bends: If a creature is more than 100 feet below the surface and ascends more than 100 feet in 1 minute, gas bubbles develop in its bloodstream from the rapid depressurization. The creature must make a Constitution saving throw at the end of that minute. The DC is 10 + 1 for every 10 feet it moved past 100 feet in 1 minute. On a failure, a creature suffers one level of exhaustion. Creatures naturally adapted to living in the ocean depths automatically succeed on this saving throw.

Cold Water: A creature more than 100 feet below the surface of the water must succeed on a DC 10 Constitution saving throw each minute or take 2 (1d4) cold damage. Creatures with resistance or immunity to cold damage or creatures naturally adapted to living in cold or deep water automatically succeed on this saving throw.

MOVING WATER

When water is moving swiftly, including rivers and rapids but also fast-moving currents and crashing surf, the following additional rules apply.

Flowing Water: Large, placid rivers move at only a few miles per hour, but some move at a swifter pace and many contain areas of rapids. A creature without a swimming speed that wades in a river treats the area as difficult terrain and has disadvantage on Dexterity (Stealth) checks. A creature that is prone in flowing water must succeed on a DC 10 Dexterity saving throw each round or be pulled 5 feet away from shore and 10 feet downstream (20 feet for fast-moving water) by the current. Creatures with a swimming speed have advantage on this saving throw.

A creature trying to swim in rapids must succeed on a DC 15 Strength (Athletics) check each round to move where it wants. Each time a creature fails this check, it is pushed up to 30 feet further down the river than where it started. Each round a creature swims through rapids, it must succeed on a DC 15 Dexterity saving throw or take 3 (1d6) bludgeoning damage. Creatures with a swimming speed have advantage on the Strength (Athletics) check and the Dexterity saving throw.

COASTAL TERRAIN

Coastal areas range from rocky cliffs to muddy tide marshes. The following special rules apply in coastal areas.

Waves: Water along the coast is difficult terrain, constantly shifting as the tides come in and out and as storms bring strong winds. A creature without a swimming speed that wades in coastal water treats the area as difficult terrain and has disadvantage on Dexterity (Stealth) checks. A creature that is prone in coastal water must succeed on a DC 10 Dexterity saving throw each round or be pulled 10 feet away from the shore by the current. Creatures with a swimming speed have advantage on this saving throw.

Strong wind, such as from a storm, causes waves to crash against the shore. Each creature in coastal water affected by a strong wind must make a DC 10 Dexterity saving throw at the end of each round. On a failed save, a creature is knocked prone and has disadvantage on the saving throw to avoid being pulled away from shore by the current.

Beaches: Beaches vary from sandy to rocky, and but while beautiful they offer dangers where the land meets the sea.

Pebbles: Some beaches are covered with broad swaths of small, loose rocks polished smooth by the action of wave and wind. Pebbles are treated as loose sand (see below), but the penalty on Dexterity checks is increased to -2.

Sand, Loose: Soft, dry sand makes it hard to keep your footing, as does extremely wet, mucky sand. Such areas are difficult terrain, and creatures in them take a -1 penalty on Dexterity checks; this penalty also applies on Dexterity saving throws to avoid being knocked prone. You can dash or charge across loose sand, but it is very tiring; if the number of times you dash or charge within 1 minute exceeds your Constitution bonus, you must make a DC 10 Constitution saving throw to avoid becoming fatigued. You can end this fatigue with a new DC 10 Constitution saving throw at the end of any round in which you do not dash, attack, cast a spell, or move more than half speed.

Sand, Packed: Wet sand is typically well-packed and comparatively easy to traverse, similar to solid ground.

Sand Dunes: Along windy coastlines, mounded dunes of loose sand are a common sight, often surmounted by tough, stringy beach grass or low-lying scrub brush undergrowth. Typical dunes are 2d6 x 10 feet long, 1d4 x 5 feet high, and 1d6 x 10 feet wide. Dunes are usually treated as loose sand, though an area with substantial undergrowth might be considered packed sand. The sloping edges of a sand dune are very difficult to climb, requiring a DC 10 Strength (Athletics) check to climb up and a DC 10 Dexterity (Acrobatics) check to climb down without falling prone. In addition, when ascending a dune each foot of movement costing 4 feet of movement when moving uphill.

Reefs: Warm seas are legendary for their bountiful and beautiful reefs teeming with sea life. Many reefs are entirely submerged, while others lie just below the surface and emerge from the water at low tide or form islets and even permanent atolls. Reefs can be miles long in total, but each reef head 1d8 x 5 feet high, usually in water 1d8 x 10 feet deep (though rare deepwater coral can be found 200 or more feet below the surface), extending 1d12 x 5 feet long and wide. Coral heads may separated by wide passes 1d4 x 10 feet wide, or narrow crevasses 5 feet wide and dropping 1d4 x 5 feet.

If the coral is within 5 feet of the surface, creatures can walk across it, treating it as difficult terrain. Such coral spans can form natural bridges from beaches to rocky offshore outcrops and may hide entrances to stony rifts or caves below the water's surface. Medium or smaller swimming creatures can move through a reef, treating it as difficult terrain, but reefs are impassable to Large or larger swimmers.

Tide Pools: These collections of seawater keep transitional zone life alive when the tide recedes and are often infested with urchins, anemones, starfish, and a variety of mollusks and crustaceans. Such creatures often are venomous, and a creature knocked prone or taking piercing or slashing damage while in a tide pool, or spending 1 minute or more prone in a tide pool becomes poisoned unless they make a DC 12 Constitution save.

Striking a Reef: A ship takes 10 (3d6) piercing damage for every 10 feet it moves within an area covered in reefs. Each reef within 5 feet of the ship is destroyed after dealing its damage to the ship. A creature with proficiency in navigator's tools or water vehicles has advantage on saving throws and ability checks to see and avoid hitting a reef. Areas covered in submerged rocks work like areas covered in reefs, except the rocks aren't destroyed after the ship moves through the area.

SHIPWRECKS

Wrecked ships are common in the oceans whether in the dark depths or crashed on a reef. Along with the danger of encountering unfriendly creatures inhabiting the wreckage, characters must also be wary of rotten wood. The timbers of a wrecked ship swell with seawater, becoming rotten and unstable. A creature must succeed on a DC 15 Wisdom (Perception) check to notice that a particular section of wood is not structurally sound. If a creature steps on the rotten wood, the wood breaks and the creature falls onto rocks or a lower deck, taking 1d6 bludgeoning damage for every 10 feet it fell. The creature must then succeed on a DC 15 Dexterity saving throw or be knocked prone and buried by the timbers that come crashing down on top of it. The buried creature is restrained and unable to stand up. A creature, including the buried target, can take an action to make a DC 10 Strength check, ending the buried state on a success.

When the pilot of a ship is navigating water filled with partially sunken wrecked ships, treat the spaces containing the wrecked ships as if they were reefs.

LIST OF CREATURES BY TYPE:

The following section lists all monsters included in this book, alphabetically by their type.

Aberration	charybdis, incutilis, jorganth, scylla
Beast	bladefish, bunyip, cephalina, crimson jellyfish, deep tiger anemone, dinichthys, dire seastar, electric eel, giant moray eel, giant squid, great white whale, hippocampus, hunter urchin, jellyfish swarm, jewel crab, lasher scallop, lasiodon, megalodon, mindclaw, ravenous urchin swarm, sapphire jellyfish, sea serpent, shipwrecker crab, slaughtermaw lamprey
Construct	cannon golem, clockwork leviathan, coral golem
Dragon	fjord linnorm, Midgard Serpent, sea drake
Elemental	ocean elemental
Fey	nereid, reef hag, selkie, storm hag
Humanoid	loran, merfolk guardian, selachim sahuagin, triton, wereshark
Monstrosity	adaro, adaro vortex-rider, asquenti, benthonir, devilfish, karkinoi, namonti benthonir, seaweed siren, siren
Ooze	globster
Plant	conch tree, living island, sargassum fiend, seaweed leshy
Undead	bone ship, draugr, draugr captain, draugr crew, duppy, sea bonze

LIST OF CREATURES BY CHALLENGE:

The following section lists all monsters included in this book, alphabetically by their Challenge level.

0	cephalina
1/4	draugr, electric eel, hippocampus, seaweed leshy
1/2	adaro, hunter urchin, lasher scallop, merfolk guardian
1	ravenous urchin swarm
2	asquenti, benthonir, draugr captain, giant moray eel, namonti benthonir, triton
3	incutilis, jewel crab, selachim sahuagin, siren
4	adaro vortex-rider, bunyip, crimson jellyfish
5	bladefish, devilfish, giant squid, globster, loran, reef hag
6	dire seastar, jellyfish swarm, karkinoi, sea drake, selkie, wereshark
7	conch tree, duppy, nereid
8	jorganth

9	coral golem, sargassum fiend
10	mindclaw, slaughtermaw lamprey
11	megalodon, sapphire jellyfish
12	clockwork leviathan, dinichthys, draugr crew, sea serpent, storm hag
13	ocean giant
14	deep tiger anemone
16	cannon golem, shipwrecker crab
17	great white whale, seaweed siren
18	bone ship, lasiodon
19	ocean elemental, sea bonze
20	living island
21	fjord linnorm
23	Scylla
30	Midgard serpent

ADARO

Malevolent denizens of the waters, adaros are among the fiercest sentient hunters of the tropical seas. They are known and feared by sailors on many exotic shores, as well as by common folk who just happen to live near the ocean. Many have witnessed a fellow sailor or fisher suddenly go rigid, a poisoned spear jutting from his guts, only to fall into the water and be taken by the vicious adaro responsible for the assault.

Ripjaw. Strictly carnivorous, adaros feed upon their victims almost immediately after slaying them. Their brutally sharp teeth cut through bone almost as easily as through flesh, and their powerful digestive systems are capable of handling most organic matter. Adaros usually eat once every couple of days, gorging on meals half their weight.

Stormchasers. Adaros' strange relationship with storms has intrigued scholars for centuries. These sea-dwellers have a special connection to the deadly creatures of the water and the wildness of foul weather, and it is no coincidence that they attack humanoids more often during rough seas. Adaros are seminomadic by nature; a tribe travels until it finds a suitable hunting ground, and leaves either when its presence becomes too well known or when its game runs low.

An adaro is 7-1/2 feet long and weighs 250 pounds.

ADARO

Medium monstrosity, neutral evil

Armor Class 14 (natural armor)

Hit Points 30 (4d10+8)

Speed 10 ft., swim 50 ft.

STR	DEX	CON	INT	WIS	CHA
15 (+2)	15 (+2)	14 (+2)	10 (+0)	13 (+1)	13 (+1)

Skills Perception +3, Stealth +4

Senses blindsense 30 ft., darkvision 60 ft.; passive Perception 13

Languages Aquan, Common

Challenge 1/2 (100 XP)

Poison Use. Adaros favor a paralytic toxin secreted by the flying nettlefin pufferfish—a sticky venom that doesn't wash away in water.

Rain Frenzy. Adaros revere storms, and their lust for blood is amplified exponentially while it is raining. While fighting in the rain or during other stormy weather, adaros have advantage on Strength saving throws and saving throws against being frightened. In such conditions, at the start of its turn, the adaro can gain advantage on all melee weapon attack rolls during that turn, but attack rolls against it have advantage until the start of its next turn. An adaro gains this benefit even if

it is underwater, but only as long as it remains within one turn away from the water's surface (50 feet for most adaros).

Speak with Sharks. An adaro can communicate telepathically with sharks to a distance of 100 feet. This communication is limited to simple concepts, such as "come," "defend," or "attack."

ACTIONS

Multiattack. The adaro makes two spear attacks. It may substitute a bite for one spear attack.

Bite. *Melee Weapon Attack:* +4 to hit, reach 5 ft., one target. *Hit:* 5 (1d6 + 2) piercing damage.

Spear. *Melee or Ranged Weapon Attack:* +4 to hit, reach 5 ft. or range 20/60 ft., one target. *Hit:* 5 (1d6 + 2) piercing damage, or 6 (1d8 + 2) piercing damage if used with two hands to make a melee attack, and the target must succeed on a DC 13 Constitution saving throw or be poisoned for 1 minute. The poisoned creature is paralyzed. The creature can repeat the saving throw at the end of each of its turns, ending the effect on itself on a success.

Adaro Vortex-Rider

Medium monstrosity, neutral evil

Armor Class 15 (natural armor)

Hit Points 120 (16d10+32)

Speed 10 ft., swim 50 ft.

STR	DEX	CON	INT	WIS	CHA
17 (+3)	15 (+2)	14 (+2)	10 (+0)	13 (+1)	17 (+3)

Skills Perception +3, Stealth +4

Senses blindsense 30 ft., darkvision 60 ft.; passive Perception 13

Languages Aquan, Common

Challenge 4 (1,100 XP)

Legendary Resistance (1/Day). If the adaro fails a saving throw, it can choose to succeed instead.

Poison Use. Adaros favor a paralytic toxin secreted by the flying nettlefin pufferfish—a sticky venom that doesn't wash away in water.

Rain Frenzy. Adaros revere storms, and their lust for blood is amplified exponentially while it is raining. While fighting in the rain or during other stormy weather, adaros have advantage on Strength saving throws and saving throws against being frightened. In such conditions, at the start of its turn, the adaro can gain advantage on all melee weapon attack rolls during that turn, but attack rolls against it have advantage until the start of its next turn. An adaro gains this benefit even if it is underwater, but only as long as it remains within one turn away from the water's surface (50 feet for most adaros).

Speak with Sharks. An adaro can communicate telepathically with sharks to a distance of 100 feet. This communication is limited to simple concepts, such as "come," "defend," or "attack."

Actions

Multiattack. The adaro makes two spear attacks. It may substitute a bite for one spear attack.

Bite. *Melee Weapon Attack:* +5 to hit, reach 5 ft., one target. *Hit:* 6 (1d6 + 3) piercing damage.

Spear. *Melee or Ranged Weapon Attack:* +5 to hit, reach 5 ft. or range 20/60 ft., one target.

Hit: 6 (1d6 + 3) piercing damage, or 7 (1d8 + 3) piercing damage if used with two hands to make a melee attack, and the target must succeed on a DC 13 Constitution saving throw or be poisoned for 1 minute. The poisoned creature is paralyzed. The creature can repeat the saving throw at the end of each of its turns, ending the effect on itself on a success.

Create Waterspout (1/Day). The adaro causes a swirling vortex of water to rise up out of any body of water it is currently in. The water rises beneath the adaro, lifting it up and providing it with a semi-stable platform of water. This waterspout allows the adaro to move above the surface of the water as thought it has a fly speed of 20 ft., and it can hover. As an action, the adaro can move through the spaces of hostile creatures during its turn, ending in an empty space. Any creature whose space the waterspout passes through, or that enters the area of the waterspout, must make a DC 13 Strength saving throw. On a failed saving throw, the target takes 7 (2d6) bludgeoning damage and is hurled 1d4 x 5 feet in a random direction into an empty space. The waterspout does not extend beneath the surface of the water. Once created, the waterspout lasts for 1 minute.

Legendary Actions

An adaro vortex-rider can take 3 legendary actions, choosing from the options below. Only one legendary action option can be used at a time and only at the end of another creature's turn. The adaro regains spent legendary actions at the start of its turn.

Detect. The adaro makes a Wisdom (Perception) check.

Spear Attack. The adaro attacks once with its spear.

Move (Costs 2 Actions). The adaro moves up to its speed without provoking opportunity attacks.

ASQUENTI

Asquenti live in the shallow upper reaches of the world's oceans, using their innate sense of the waters around them to hunt for prey with their sonic lance. Once a foe is stunned, asquenti swarm them and finish them off with pincers, hoping to keep them stunned and non-resistant. As apex predators, they have undisputed dominance of their territories.

Asquenti colonies can have several thousand residents, and create wondrous coral cities, coaxing the living coral into useful structures. Scholars and technologists use a combination of subsonic frequencies and their knowledge of the marine world to rapidly increase coral growth and grow buildings in a matter of weeks. Asquenti colonies regularly patrol their territories, ensuring their food isn't poached by others, as well as looking out for kraken agents lurking in the depths.

Toxin Intolerance. Their sense of the natural world around them is particularly sensitive to foreign technological or magical pollutants. Not only do these threaten their habitat and their food sources, but an excess of pollutants in their waters catalyzes biochemical reactions in asquenti. These changes affect their psychology to be more militant, and inflame their passions, causing them to attack the cause of the disruption. While this doesn't turn asquenti into mindless killing machines, it does strengthen their martial instincts, causing most asquenti to become aggressive to all outsiders. Most asquenti assume land dwellers pollute their waters, and even when their home waters are pristine, asquenti have an innate distrust of land dwellers. Persistent peaceful overtures can overcome this distrust, especially in the asquenti who fail to succumb to their biochemical drives.

A typical asquenti stands 7 feet tall and weighs 500 pounds.

ASQUENTI

Medium monstrosity, neutral

Armor Class 13 (natural armor)

Hit Points 45 (6d8 + 18)

Speed 20 ft., swim 60 ft.

STR	DEX	CON	INT	WIS	CHA
14 (+2)	14 (+2)	16 (+3)	10 (+0)	12 (+1)	8 (-1)

Skills Nature +2, Survival +3

Damage Resistances thunder

Senses darkvision 60 ft., incredible sight, passive Perception 11

Languages Asquenti, Aquan

Challenge 2 (450 XP)

Incredible Sight. The asquenti's eyes pick up colors well beyond human range, and it can see perfectly in all light conditions. As long as it is not blinded, it is treated as if it has blindsight out to 60 feet.

Water Breathing. The asquenti can breathe only underwater.

ACTIONS

Multiattack. The asquenti makes two attacks with its claws.

Claw. Melee Weapon Attack. +4 to hit, reach 5 ft., one target. *Hit:* 5 (1d6 + 2) bludgeoning damage

Sonic Lance. Ranged Weapon Attack. +4 to hit, range 100 ft., one target. *Hit:* 5 (1d6 + 2) thunder damage, and the target must succeed on a DC 13 Constitution saving throw or be stunned for 1 round.

Sonic Pincer. Melee Weapon Attack. +4 to hit, reach 5 ft., one target. *Hit:* 5 (1d6+2) bludgeoning damage plus 5 (1d6 + 2) thunder damage, and the target must succeed on a DC 13 Constitution saving throw or be stunned for 1 round.

BENTHONIR

Endemic to deepest parts of the ocean, benthonir are transparent humanoids with an undifferentiated biology. Each drop of the condensed slime that makes up a benthonir's body is interchangeable with the rest so long as enough of the body remains viable to maintain life. This extends to the beginning of their lives, with vast fields of benthonir buds growing on the walls of ocean trenches.

Kraken Cultists. Vast schools of benthonir gather in the trenches. There they worship the krakens they believe created them from the lesser creatures of the trenches and, at the krakens' behest, wage war on the asquenti realms above. In their pantheon, the krakens only bend knee to the even greater Vulnatatoa.

Mutations. With their great numbers and ever-shifting form, it comes as no surprise that the benthonir are susceptible to a wide variety of mutations. Few surface dwellers have seen a normal benthonir and fewer still recognize them as kin to the mutants who can be found on the surface. Thankfully for surface dwellers, the benthonir can only bud in the trenches, leaving the surface as yet uninvaded.

Fire Shark benthonirs have red coloration that gathers in scales over their transparent flesh. This appearance grants them advantage on Dexterity (Stealth) checks while in the vast kelp jungles below he waves. They are also immune to fire rather than cold and often have multiple arms.

Human Born benthonirs look completely human but lose fast healing and their swim speed, instead gaining a normal 30-foot land speed. They can suppress their bite, claw, and morphic form as a bonus action. Using these abilities can reveal their true nature, but otherwise detecting their benthoniri biology requires close examination requiring at least 1 hour and a successful DC 20 Intelligence (Nature) check.

Human Mimic benthonirs look like incomplete human beings, wrinkled as their flesh constantly melts and reforms, but could be mistaken for elderly humans in poor light. They have a land speed of 30 feet and a swim speed of 20 feet.

Namonti benthonirs look like asquenti and can only be distinguished with a cursory medical examination (Wisdom (Medicine) DC 10) or scoring a critical hit on them in combat. They also possess the base asquenti pincer, sonic lance, and sonic pincer attacks rather than their claw and bite.

BENTHONIR
Medium monstrosity, neutral

Armor Class 13

Hit Points 71 (11d8 + 22)

Speed 20 ft., swim 40 ft.

STR	DEX	CON	INT	WIS	CHA
16 (+3)	16 (+3)	14 (+2)	9 (-1)	10 (+0)	10 (+0)

Skills Athletics +5, Stealth +5

Damage Immunities cold

Senses blindsense 30 ft., darkvision 60 ft., passive Perception 10

Languages Aquan, Benthoniri

Challenge 2 (450 XP)

Regeneration. The benthonir regains 5 hit points at the start of its turn if it has at least 1 hit point.

Water Breathing. The benthonir can breathe air and water. Additionally, a benthonir can freely cast spells and use other abilities while submerged.

ACTIONS

Multiattack. The benthonir makes two attacks: one with its bite and one with its claw.

Bite. *Melee Weapon Attack.* +5 to hit, reach 5 ft., one target. *Hit:* 7 (1d8 + 3) slashing damage.

Claw. *Melee Weapon Attack.* +5 to hit, reach 5 ft., one target. *Hit:* 6 (1d6 + 3) bludgeoning damage.

NAMONTI BENTHONIR

Medium monstrosity, neutral

Armor Class 12

Hit Points 71 (11d8 + 22)

Speed 20 ft., swim 40 ft.

STR	DEX	CON	INT	WIS	CHA
14 (+2)	14 (+2)	14 (+2)	9 (-1)	10 (+0)	10 (+0)

Skills Athletics +4, Stealth +4

Damage Immunities cold

Senses blindsense 30 ft., darkvision 60 ft., passive Perception 10

Languages Aquan, Benthoniri

Challenge 2 (450 XP)

Regeneration. The benthonir regains 5 hit points at the start of its turn if it has at least 1 hit point.

Water Breathing. The benthonir can breathe air and water. Additionally, a benthonir can freely cast spells and use other abilities while submerged.

Asquenti Mimic. The namonti benthonir looks like an asquenti and can only be distinguished with a cursory medical examination (Wisdom (Medicine) DC 10) or by scoring a critical hit against it.

ACTIONS

Multiattack. The namonti benthonir makes two attacks: one with its bite and one with its claw.

Claw. Melee Weapon Attack. +4 to hit, reach 5 ft., one target. *Hit:* 5 (1d6 + 2) bludgeoning damage.

Sonic Lance. Ranged Weapon Attack. +4 to hit, range 60/180 ft., one target. *Hit:* 5 (1d6 + 2) thunder damage, and the target must succeed on a DC 12 Constitution saving throw or be stunned for 1 round.

Sonic Pincer. Melee Weapon Attack. +4 to hit, reach 5 ft., one target. *Hit:* 5 (1d6 + 2) bludgeoning damage plus 5 (2d4) thunder damage, and the target must succeed on a DC 12 Constitution saving throw or be stunned for 1 round.

BONE SHIP

Predators of the oceans, the hulking undead monstrosities known as bone ships leave devastation in their bloody wakes. Formed from the collective consciousnesses of dead sailors bound within the bleached bones of giant aquatic creatures, bone ships hunt the seas without mercy, destroying ships and slaying the living wherever they are encountered. Bone ships stalk their prey with tenacious intelligence and single-minded purpose. They often trail their quarry for days, relishing the terror their sudden appearance on the horizon causes, and have even been known to continue the chase on land, the many bones of their hulls pulling them over the ground. Bone ships do not care for plunder, seeking only to add more victims to their unholy crews.

The creation of a bone ship can occur in many different ways. Some bone ships arise as servants of evil gods, pawns to their vile wills. Certain powerful necromantic rituals can also create bone ships. Such rituals typically require those performing them to sacrifice dozens of humanoid creatures and trap the victims' souls. Other bone ships result from ships being destroyed in horrific and catastrophic events. The souls of the sailors who died in such a disaster, unable to find peace, slowly form a bone ship on the ocean's bottom before rising to the surface to take vengeance on the living. No matter how they're created, bone ships retain jumbled memories of the previous lives of the souls bound to them—though all bone ships attack any creatures they encounter, each ship's unique origin and collection of souls burns a particular objective into its very nature. A bone ship created by an evil god might target ships bearing the flags of an opposing faith or enemy of that god, while a bone ship created in a ritual is ingrained with a specific purpose that forces it to enact its creator's will. Certain bone ships viciously target ships from one or more nations, either those from the dead sailors' former nation if they seek revenge, or those from a rival nation the sailors hated in life.

Over time, legends and stories about a bone ship's capacity for destruction arise. A bone ship never takes a name for itself but living sailors may ascribe it an epithet based on its origin, purpose, unique characteristics, or notable attacks. Though all bone ships possess the same abilities, a particular bone ship can be identified by its hunting area and appearance. Bone ships eventually display certain unique features such as glowing barnacles that cover its hull, a masthead featuring the skull of a particular sea creature, the bones of a unique and rare sea monster, or an unusual configuration of the musculature holding together its hull. Many of these changes are the result of a bone ship scavenging remains off the ocean floor to repair itself.

Lone Ships. No living crew—or even other undead creatures—have ever been seen sailing in a bone ship. These undead ships operate independently, and don't form alliances even with others of their kind. Merely attempting to communicate with a bone ship is dangerous, as even such means as telepathy produce only the howling voices of the suffering, ghostly crew, spreading their insanity to those foolish enough to contact them.

Modular Shape. Though a bone ship is a single creature, the numerous souls it contains create a hive mind. A bone ship can reshape certain aspects of its hull by using its knotted muscle to move the bones within it. This transformative ability allows a bone ship to quickly sprout cannons from its hull that can attack in any direction, and each ship keeps a collection of bones and debris within its own body to use as ammunition. It can also tap into the unholy energy giving it unlife to fire a devastating beam of negative energy at its enemies, and those who close with a bone ship find that even its hull has the ability to drain away life force.

BONE SHIP

Gargantuan undead, chaotic evil

Armor Class 18 (natural armor)

Hit Points 297 (17d20+119)

Speed swim 60 ft.

STR	DEX	CON	INT	WIS	CHA
28 (+9)	16 (+3)	24 (+7)	11 (+0)	17 (+3)	19 (+4)

Saving Throws Str +15, Con +13, Wis +9

Damage Resistances necrotic

Damage Immunities poison

Condition Immunities charmed, exhausted, frightened, poisoned

Senses darkvision 100 ft.; passive Perception 13

Languages Common (can't speak)

Challenge 18 (20,000 XP)

Blood Wake. The frothing, churning waters around a bone ship are stained crimson with blood. Creatures that begin theit turn within 40 feet of the bone ship must make DC 18 Constitution saves. Those that fail become frightened. Targets that are frightened cannot use reactions and can use either an action on their turn or a bonus action, not both. Creatures can attempt a new save at the start of each of their turns to resist this effect. Those that succeed at their saving throws are immune to the bone ship's aura for 24 hours. This works only when the bone ship is in the water.

Bound Souls. The souls of numerous sailors and sea creatures form the bone ship's collective consciousness and hull. A bone ship is immune to spells and effects affecting a specific number of creatures. Any creature attempting to communicate with a bone ship, such as through telepathy, hears only the anguished cries of the imprisoned souls and must succeed at a DC 18 Wisdom save or contract long-term madness.

Turn Resistance. The bone ship has advantage on saving throws against any effect that turns undead.

Unholy Repair. By spending 1 full day inactive, the bone ship can heal itself to full hit points by scavenging the bones of dead sea creatures within a 10-mile radius, pulling the bones up from the bottom of the ocean to join its hull.

ACTIONS

Multiattack. The bone ship attacks four times with bone cannons.

Slam. *Melee Weapon Attack:* +15 to hit, reach 5 ft., one target. *Hit:* 45 (8d8+9) bludgeoning damage, and the target must succeed at a DC 18 Constitution saving throw or take 10 (3d6) necrotic damage.

Bone Cannon. *Ranged Weapon Attack:* +15 to hit, range 100/400 ft., one target. *Hit:* 30 (6d6+9) bludgeoning damage. The cannons are considered to be part of the bone ship and not separate objects.

Ghostly Boarders (Recharge 6). The bone ship disgorges the souls of the sailors bound within it. The ghostly boarders appear as spectral entities and slaughter all living creatures in a 60-foot sphere around the bone ship. Each creature in that area must make a DC 18 Constitution saving throw. A target takes 28 (8d6) necrotic damage on a failed save, or half as much damage on a successful one. Creatures reduced to 0 hit points in this manner are killed, their souls dragged into the bone ship, and can be restored to life only by a *wish* spell, or if the bone ship is destroyed.

Spectral Energy Cannon (Recharge 4-6). The bone ship can combine all four of its bone cannons into a spectral energy cannon, blasting a line 100 feet long and 5 feet wide. Each creature in the line must make a DC 18 Dexterity saving throw. A creature takes 63 (18d6) necrotic damage on a failed save, or half as much damage on a successful one.

BUNYIP

The bunyip is a fierce and avid hunter, possessing a primal ruthlessness that seems almost evil in its rapacity. A bunyip typically inhabits large freshwater inlets, marshy sloughs and bayous, or sheltered coastal sea caves where food is plentiful—the bunyip is equally at home in fresh or salt water. It prefers feeding on animals of Small size or larger, though it isn't averse to eating humanoids when presented the opportunity. Bunyips are quite territorial, and readily attack when intruders threaten their hunting grounds. Bunyips mate annually, during the late spring. During this period, bunyips become even more aggressive. After mating, couples split, with the female wandering off to find a place to birth a small litter of four to six pups. Females watch their pups for a few days, until they become independent enough for the mothers to move on.

Adaptable. Reports of bunyip sightings come from every end of the map. Though the accuracy of all such reports remains doubtful, enough reliable accounts exist to confirm their widespread adaptability. The species thrives in numerous ecological climes, from frigid polar fjords to idyllic tropical lagoons. The bunyip is not a deep-sea creature, and even avoids larger freshwater lakes, as it prefers to lurk near shorelines where its favorite food is more common.

Bunyips vary in appearance as much as they do in their habitat. All possess a similar physical structures to a large seal, with an oversized mouth filled with sharp fangs. All bunyips have at least a thin layer of hair, generally longer and shaggier in freshwater bunyips, and usually in shades of pale gray, brown, or black.

While bunyips can survive equally well in fresh or salt water, those dwelling in the ocean have developed somewhat differently from their cousins that live close to land. Oceangoing bunyips usually have a thick, muscular tail ending in wide flukes and jaws that seem almost shark-like. Their flippered forelimbs are strong and sharp-edged, while their rear flippers are vestigial and weak.

Freshwater bunyips by contrast have vaguely canine heads, often with large fangs or even tusks. Their tails are long but much slimmer, with very small flukes sometimes covered in a tuft of hair. However, they retain four strong flippered limbs, splayed like webbed fingers and tipped with stubby claws, and have proven to be surprisingly clever and dextrous in using them.

BUNYIP

Medium monstrosity, unaligned

Armor Class 14 (natural armor)

Hit Points 112 (15d8 + 45)

Speed 10 ft., swim 50 ft.

STR	DEX	CON	INT	WIS	CHA
13 (+1)	16 (+3)	13 (+1)	2 (−4)	11 (+0)	7 (−2)

Saving Throws Dex +5

Skills Stealth +5

Senses darkvision 60 ft., passive Perception 10

Languages —

Challenge 4 (1,100 XP)

Blood Frenzy. If a creature takes piercing or slashing damage within 30 feet of the bunyip while they are both swimming, or if the bunyip is damaged, the bunyip goes into a frenzy for 1 minute, gaining advantage on all attack rolls.

Water Breathing. The bunyip can only breathe underwater.

ACTIONS

Bite. Melee Weapon Attack. +5 to hit, 5 ft. reach, one target. *Hit:* 23 (4d10 + 1) piercing damage.

Horrifying Roar. A bunyip's roar is supernaturally loud and horrifying. When a bunyip roars, all hearing creatures within 100 feet must succeed on a DC 14 Wisdom saving throw to avoid being deafened and frightened. A deafened creature can attempt a DC 14 Constitution saving throw at the end of each of its turns to end the effect. A frightened creature can attempt a DC 14 Wisdom saving throw at he end of each of its turns to end the effect. Whether or not the initial saving throw is successful, creatures in the area are immune to the roar of that bunyip for 24 hours.

CEPHALINA

Cephalina are tiny, nautilus-like creatures native to the shallow warm or temperate ocean waters. They are herbivores, feeding on algae and other waterborne microscopic life. Cephalina navigate in the dark by creation of luminous ink that they use to illuminate dark spaces. Typically, these tiny creatures dwell at near-surface levels and venture up onto the shore to scrape algae off of rocks as tides lower.

A cephalina measures about 1 foot across and weighs 6 lbs.

Farmed Ink. Cephalina are often raised in captivity by both aquatic and surface races, and their ink is harvested to create phosphorescent dyes and pigments.

CEPHALINA

Tiny beast, unaligned

Armor Class 12

Hit Points 3 (2d4 - 2)

Speed 20 ft., swim 20 ft.

STR	DEX	CON	INT	WIS	CHA
2 (-4)	14 (+2)	8 (-1)	3 (-4)	12 (+1)	12 (+1)

Senses darkvision 30 ft., passive Perception 11

Languages -

Challenge 0 (10 XP)

Amphibious. The cephalina can breathe air or water.

Familiar Suitability. At the GM's discretion, the spell find familiar may summon a familiar that resembles a cephalina.

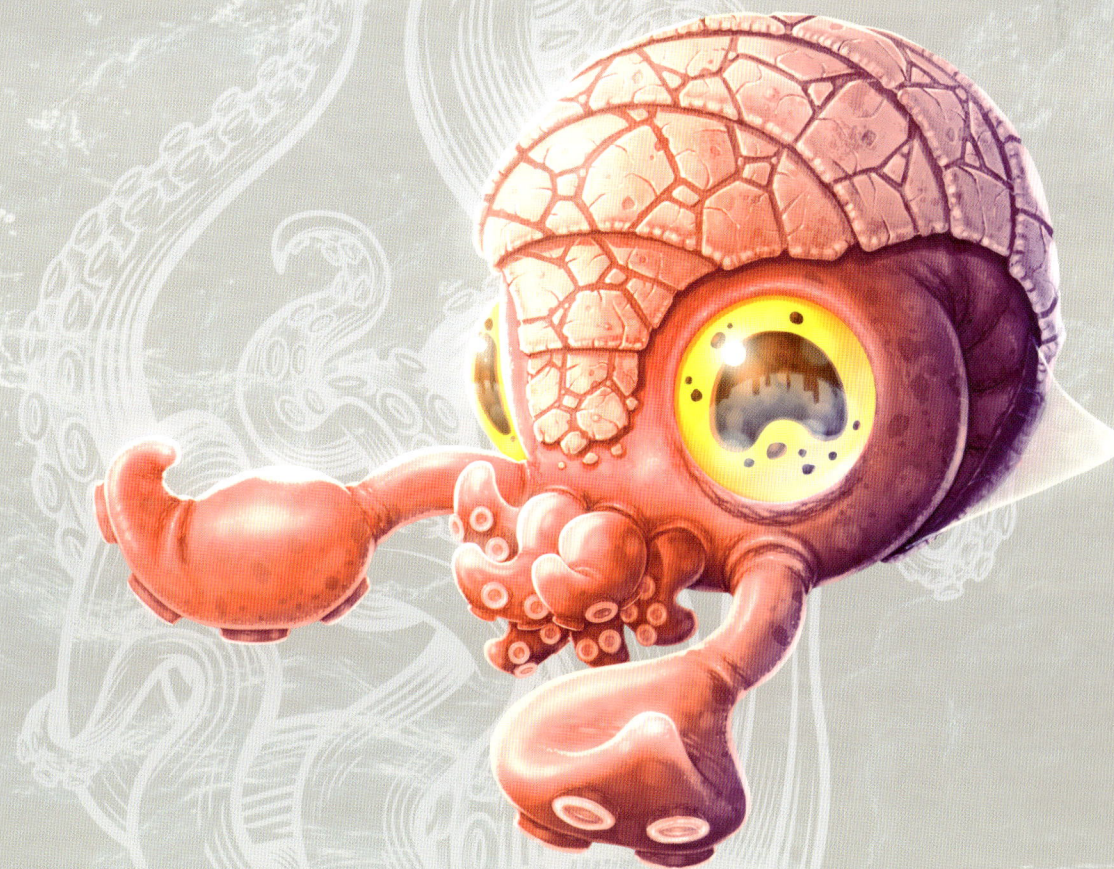

ACTIONS

Tentacle. Melee Weapon Attack: +0 to hit, reach 5 ft., one target. *Hit:* 1 bludgeoning damage.

Ink. Underwater, the cephalina can squirt a tiny cloud of luminous pink ink. This ink cloud heavily obscures a 5-foot cube adjacent to the cephalia and sheds vibrant pink light like a torch for 1 round.

Spray Ink. The cephalina chooses one target within 5 feet it can see that is out of water and sprays ink at it. The target must make a DC 12 Dexterity saving throw. On a failed saving throw, the target glows with a soft, pink glow similar to torch light that imposes disadvantage on Dexterity (Stealth) checks until the end of the cephalina's next turn.

CHARYBDIS

Sailors tell many tales of the creatures of the deep, from the terrible kraken to the beautiful mermaid. Yet few are stranger or more feared than the dread charybdis, for it exists to capture ships, crack them open like nuts, and feast on the doomed sailors within. So legendary are these violent attacks that many sailors have come to view the charybdis not as a species of aberrant life, but as the vengeful personification of an angry sea god. A charybdis is 60 feet long and weighs 26,000 pounds.

Living Maelstrom. In truth, the charybdis is not the sending of an angry deity, but in fact little more than a monstrous predator capable of churning even the calmest of seas into a whirling maelstrom. The charybdis uses this vortex ability not only to capture prey like sharks or small whales, but also to entrap ships on the ocean surface above.

Shipwrecker. A charybdis' claws are particularly well suited to puncturing the hulls of ships, and most charybdises have learned that a single large merchant vessel contains enough sailors to make a perfectly sized meal. Often, a charybdis settles in along a well-known shipping route near the shoreline or amid an archipelago of islands where ships are forced along relatively narrow lanes between rocky isles—such locations allow the charybdis to lie in wait and increases the chance of its prey being unable to circumvent its vortex.

CHARYBDIS

Gargantuan aberration, unaligned

Armor Class 20 (natural armor)

Hit Points 351 (18d20+162)

Speed 20 ft., swim 50 ft.

STR	DEX	CON	INT	WIS	CHA
30 (+10)	9 (-1)	28 (+9)	4 (-3)	15 (+2)	6 (-2)

Saving Throws Str +16, Dex +5, Cha +4

Skills Athletics +16, Perception +8

Damage Resistances cold; bludgeoning, piercing, and slashing from nonmagical attacks

Damage Immunities acid

Condition Immunities frightened, prone

Senses blindsight 60 ft., darkvision 200 ft., passive Perception 18

Languages Aquan

Challenge 19 (22,000 XP)

Amphibious. The charybdis can breathe water and air.

Innate Spellcasting. The charybdis's spellcasting ability is Wisdom (spell save DC 16). It can innately cast the following spells, requiring no material components:

At will: *control water, fog cloud*

1/day each: *control weather, hallucinatory terrain*

Regeneration. The charybdis regains 10 hit points at the start of its turn if it has at least 1 hit point.

Ship Eater. The charybdis deals double damage to objects and structures.

ACTIONS

Multiattack. The charybdis makes two attacks: one with its bite, and one with its claws.

Bite. *Melee Weapon Attack:* +16 to hit, reach 10 ft., one target. *Hit:* 36 (4d12 + 10) piercing damage. If the target is a Huge or smaller creature, it must succeed on a DC 19 Strength saving throw or be swallowed by the charybdis. A swallowed creature is blinded and restrained, it has total cover against attacks and other effects outside the charybdis, and it takes 24 (7d6) acid damage at the start of each of the charybdis's turns. If the charybdis takes 40 damage or more on a single turn from a creature inside it, the charybdis must succeed on a DC 26 Constitution saving throw at the end of that turn or regurgitate all swallowed creatures, which fall prone in a space within 10 feet of the charybdis. If charybdis dies, a swallowed creature is no longer restrained by it and can escape from the corpse by using 10 feet of movement, exiting prone.

Claws. *Melee Weapon Attack:* +16 to hit, reach 30 ft., one target. *Hit:* 21 (2d10 + 10) piercing damage.

Vortex (Recharge 4–6). The charybdis draws creatures and ships within 100 feet of it in the water towards it by creating a massive whirlpool. Ships attempting to avoid this require someone at the helm of the ship must make a relevant check (usually a water vehicle proficiency) with a DC of 20, or be drawn 50 feet closer to the charybdis. Creatures in the water must make a similar Strength (Athletics) check to avoid being drawn close 25 feet. Any creature or ship that is drawn to within 10 feet or closer of the charybdis is subject to a claw attack as part of the Vortex action.

LEGENDARY ACTIONS

The charybdis can take two legendary actions, choosing from the options below. Only one legendary action option can be used at a time and only at the end of another creature's turn. The charybdis regains spent legendary actions at the start of its turn.

Claws. The charybdis makes one attack with its claws.

Control Water. The charybdis casts *control water* or chooses one the effects of *control water*.

CRABS

Jewel crabs dwell within the coastal waters and spend much of their time wandering around the ocean floor in search for prey or things to decorate their shells, using strands of naturally produced adhesive resin. While jewel crabs are aquatic, they occasionally wander out of the water in search for decorations that wash up along the shores. They are usually not aggressive towards humanoids, but they will fight if they feel threatened or if they spot something interesting to decorate their shells in the possession of a humanoid. They are typically four or five feet tall and weigh about two hundred pounds, with their shells easily making up half of that weight. Jewel crabs typically live for about thirty years in the wild, with those being kept in captivity generally only living for about fifteen years.

Hermit Home. Jewel crabs have two large claws that are fairly precise despite their size and strength, eight segmented legs for movement, and a long spirally curved asymmetrical abdomen, which is soft and vulnerable to attack, unlike the shelled abdomens seen in other crustaceans. To protect their soft abdomen, they typically salvage an empty seashell from another creature, using it like armor and turning it into a comfortable place to hide by retreating inside of it, while using its claws as a door to block the entrance. A jewel crab's body is pinkish in their immature state, shifting to dark blue in color as it matures, with glowing neon-blue accents. As they grow in size, they quickly become cramped inside their shell. Whenever a jewel crab outgrows their shell, they are forced to find another. A jewel crab outside of its shell only has a natural AC of only 11.

Decorated Shell. Despite their biological need to change shells as they grow in size, they seem to be fairly picky about what they use; favoring the shells of sea snails, but scarcity can occasionally force them to use the shells of bivalves and scaphopods (or even hollow pieces of wood and stone) in a pinch. In particularly lean times where there are not many other options available, some naturalist philosophers have observed bullying other jewel crabs for their shells and it is not too uncommon to see two of them fighting over any appropriately sized shells with surprising fury should they find it at the same time. They seem to be quite vain about their shells, constantly decorating them with new bits of collected foliage, stones, and crystals. No two shells are identical, but all are heavily decorated with chunks of crystal that give them their name. Ironically, their apparent love for decorating their shells can also lead to problems, as their shells can grow too heavy under the load of so many decorations, which often leads them to abandoning their current shell for a new one.

JEWEL CRAB

Medium beast, unaligned

Armor Class 15 (natural armor)

Hit Points 71 (11d8+22)

Speed 30 ft., burrow 15 ft., swim 15 ft.

STR	DEX	CON	INT	WIS	CHA
16 (+3)	10 (+0)	14 (+2)	2 (-4)	12 (+1)	13 (+1)

Skills Athletics +5, Perception +3, Stealth +2, Survival +5

Damage Resistance cold

Damage Immunities poison

Senses darkvision 60 ft., passive Perception 13

Languages -

Challenge 3 (700 XP)

Keen Smell. The jewel crab has advantage on Wisdom (Perception) checks that rely on smell.

Retraction. A jewel crab can pull its fleshy parts into its shell as a bonus action, allowing the jewel crab to use its shell as three-quarters cover. While retracted into its shell the jewel crab cannot move or attack. A jewel crab may reemerge from its shell by using its action.

Water Dependency. A jewel crab can survive out of the water for 1 hour per point of Constitution. After that, a jewel crab begins suffocating.

ACTIONS

Multiattack. The jewel crab makes up to 2 claw attacks, 2 resin strand attacks, or any combination thereof:

Claw. *Melee Weapon Attack:* +5 to hit, reach 5 ft., one target. *Hit:* 10 (2d6 + 3) bludgeoning damage.

Resin Strand. Ranged Weapon Attack: +5 to hit, range 30 ft., one target. *Hit:* A Large or smaller creature hit must succeed on a DC 13 Dexterity saving throw or become grappled by the jewel crab (escape DC 15), with the grapple ending automatically if the target is moved further than 30 ft. away from the jewel crab. The jewel crab may, instead of moving, drag a grappled target 15 ft. towards it. A jewel crab can maintain a maximum of 2 targets grappled by resin strands at a given time. Any acid damage inflicted on a target grappled by the jewel crab dissolves the resin and ends the grapple.

MINDCLAW

A red-brown crab the size of a wagon scuttles forward with an unusual amount of aggression.

Echoes of a Sunken Empire. Mindclaws retain the psychic impressions of countless dead, unknown centuries after the cataclysmic demise of ancient antediluvian civilizations. They behave like mindless crabs most of the time, but their simple nervous systems process powerful emotions and are easily influenced by magic. An adult mindclaw is 15 feet tall and weighs 4,000 pounds.

MINDCLAW CRAB

Huge beast, unaligned

Armor Class 21 (natural armor)

Hit Points 204 (24d12 + 48)

Speed 30 ft., swim 30 ft.

STR	DEX	CON	INT	WIS	CHA
17 (+3)	15 (+2)	14 (+2)	1 (-5)	9 (-1)	3 (-4)

Skills Perception +3, Stealth +6

Condition Immunities charmed, frightened, stunned (if it is from a psychic-based attack)

Senses blindsight 30 ft., passive Perception 13

Languages —

Challenge 10 (5,900 XP)

Amphibious. The mindclaw can breathe air and water.

Shared Empathy. Mindclaws gain any bonuses or penalties from emotion effects affecting creatures within 30 feet. The specifics are at the GM's discretion, however, by way of example a mindclaw would gain the benefits of barbarian rage if a raging barbarian was within range. A mind crab can only benefit

from the same spell or effect once regardless of bonus type or number of creatures affected by a single effect, but mindclaws do gain bonuses and penalties from other mindclaws within 30 feet. Mindclaws cannot be the target of an emotion effect (for example the *calm emotions* spell), but do not gain saving throws against emotion effects affecting other creatures.

ACTIONS

Multiattack. The mindclaw makes 2 claw attacks.

Claw. Melee Weapon Attack: +7 to hit, reach 15 ft., one target. *Hit:* 10 (2d6 + 3) bludgeoning damage and 35 (10d6) psychic damage, and the target is grappled (escape DC 17). The mindclaw has two claws, each of which can grapple only one target.

SHIPWRECKER CRAB

A bane to all vessels traveling the seas, shipwrecker crabs can ruin the career of a merchant captain in minutes, destroying her ship, dumping its cargo into the waters below, and plucking her drowning crew from the wreckage for food. Shipwrecker crabs live most of their lives in shallow seas, coming near the coast or surface to hunt and feed. A shipwrecker crab measures 50 feet across, with two long arms capable of extending a further 30 feet each and weighs 6 tons.

SHIPWRECKER CRAB

Gargantuan beast, unaligned

Armor Class 18 (natural armor)

Hit 297 (17d20+119)

Speed 30 ft., swim 40 ft.

STR	DEX	CON	INT	WIS	CHA
24 (+7)	16 (+3)	24 (+7)	2 (-4)	14 (+2)	5 (-3)

Saving Throws Str +12, Con +12

Skills Athletics +12, Perception +7

Senses darkvision 60 ft., passive Perception 17

Languages –

Challenge 16 (15,000 XP)

Angled Carapace. Ranged weapon attacks made with non-magical weapons have disadvantage against the shipwrecker crab.

Improved Critical. The shipwrecker crab scores a critical hit on a roll of 19 or 20.

Siege Monster. The shipwrecker crab deals double damage to objects and structures.

Water Breathing. The shipwrecker crab can only breathe underwater.

ACTIONS

Multiattack. The shipwrecker crab makes two claw attacks.

Claw. Melee Weapon Attack. +12 to hit, 20 ft. reach, one target. *Hit:* 51 (8d10 + 7) bludgeoning damage.

CLOCKWORK LEVIATHAN

Clockwork leviathans are massive eel-like metallic dragons with two webbed talons and tails ending in large, powerful flukes. They are equally capable of functioning on land and in water. Sailors who are haunted by the memories of these treacherous machines need not exaggerate their yarns, for the reality of an aquatic construct such as this holds enough terror in its story for even the hardiest of seafarers. A clockwork leviathan's numerous metal plates and links are made of such resilient material that they never rust, even after long exposure to the briny sea waters that leviathans often patrol. Clockwork leviathans are 25 feet long and weigh over 3 tons.

Clockwork. As a constructed being, a clockwork leviathan doesn't eat, breathe, drink, or sleep. If it is not wound, it eventually becomes inert until it is wound again.

CLOCKWORK LEVIATHAN

Huge construct, unaligned

Armor Class 21 (natural armor)

Hit Points 171 (18d12+54)

Speed 30 ft., swim 60 ft.

STR	DEX	CON	INT	WIS	CHA
23 (+6)	18 (+4)	16 (+3)	1 (-5)	11 (+0)	1 (-5)

Damage Immunities fire, poison, psychic

Damage Resistance bludgeoning, piercing, and slashing from nonmagical attacks that aren't adamantine

Damage Vulnerabilities lightning

Condition Immunities charmed, exhaustion, frightened, paralyzed, petrified, poisoned

Senses darkvision 120 ft.; passive Perception 10

Languages understands the languages of its creator but can't speak

Challenge 12 (8,400 XP)

Winding. A clockwork leviathan can function for two weeks every time it is wound. A creature of at least Medium size can use an action to wind the clockwork soldier, restoring to it 1 hour of operating time; a creature of Small size can wind it at half this speed, and Tiny or smaller creatures are generally unable to wind the leviathan.

ACTIONS

Multiattack. The clockwork leviathan makes two attacks: one with its bite and one constrict.

Bite. *Melee Weapon Attack*: +10 to hit, reach 10 ft., one target. *Hit*: 13 (2d6 + 6) piercing damage.

Constrict. *Melee weapon attack*: +10 to hit, reach 5 ft., one target. *Hit*: 15 (2d8 + 6) bludgeoning damage and 22 (4d10) slashing damage, and the target is grappled (escape DC 20). Until this grapple ends, the creature is restrained, and the clockwork leviathan can't constrict another target.

Steam Breath (Recharge 5–6). The clockwork leviathan exhales scorching steam in a 60-foot line that is 5 feet wide. Each creature in that line must make a DC 15 Dexterity saving throw, taking 54 (12d8) fire damage on a failed save, or half as much damage on a successful one. A clockwork leviathan's breath weapon functions equally well above and under water.

Conch Tree

Conch trees are frequently cultivated as living barriers, unsporting hedges against unwanted incursions. After centuries of breeding and experimentation, they developed an instinct for discerning regular travellers among their groves from visiting prey. In the wild, entire schools of fish can vanish instantly over a conch grove.

Cadaverous Reproduction. Conch trees reproduce by implanting a single seed in a partially digested corpse. The corpse is then expelled so the seed can absorb nutrients before sprouting and taking root. Conch trees never stop growing, but an average adult specimen is 20 feet tall.

Conch Tree

Large plant, unaligned

Armor Class 16 (natural armor)

Hit Points 94 (9d10 + 45)

Speed 0 ft.

STR	DEX	CON	INT	WIS	CHA
23 (+6)	8 (-1)	21 (+5)	1 (-5)	16 (+3)	1 (-5)

Damage Resistances bludgeoning, piercing

Damage Vulnerabilities fire

Senses blindsight 60 ft., passive Perception 13

Languages –

Challenge 7 (2,900 XP)

False Appearance. While the conch tree remains motionless, it is indistinguishable from a normal seaweed bed.

Water Breathing. The conch tree can breathe only underwater.

Actions

Multiattack. The conch tree makes two harpoon tentacle attacks.

Harpoon Tentacle. Melee or Ranged Weapon Attack: +9 to hit, reach 5 ft. or range 60 ft., one target. *Hit:* 28 (4d10 + 6) piercing damage. If the target is a Medium or smaller creature, it must succeed on a DC 15 Dexterity saving throw or be reeled into the seaweed mass that makes up the conch tree and are swallowed whole. This triggers the collapse ability of the conch tree. A swallowed creature is blinded and restrained, it has total cover against attacks and other effects outside the worm, and it takes 7 (2d6) bludgeoning and 3 (1d6) acid damage at the start of each of the conch tree's turns. If the conch tree takes 10 damage or more on a single turn from a creature inside it, the conch tree must succeed on a DC 17 Constitution saving throw at the end of that turn or regurgitate all swallowed creatures, which fall prone in a space within 10 feet of the tree. If the tree dies, a swallowed creature is no longer restrained by it and can escape from the corpse by using 20 feet of movement, exiting prone.

Reaction

Collapse. Once a conch tree swallows a creature whole, it can collapse into a smaller hard shell to protect itself while it digests its prey. The tree curls around its prey, reinforcing its own outer flesh and changing colors to represent mud or stone. It gains a damage threshold of 10 and a +20 bonus on Dexterity (Stealth) checks while on the ocean floor.

DEVILFISH

Although the devilfish superficially resembles a purplish cephalopod with a swarm of slashing spined arms, most often seven but some with as many as 13. These slashing arms are shaded a mottled blue, as are its octopoid eyes, though it sometimes retreats into a nautiloid shell. While it might appear to be simply a strange sort of octopus or squid, a devilfish is an altogether different creature with a heritage steeped in the lower planes. A devilfish is 10 feet long and weighs 500 pounds.

Fiendish Cunning. More than those of a mere animal, the devilfish's intelligence and several of its abilities are gifts from a fiendish legacy—most sages believe that the original devilfish were once fiends from the Abyss, and that over the course of thousands of years they became true natives of the Material Plane's oceans. Possessing a rudimentary intellect, a devilfish can understand and even speak a few words and phrases in various languages, although when it speaks, it has a tendency to mix languages together, making it somewhat difficult to understand for anyone who doesn't speak all the languages known by the devilfish.

Rumors of far more intelligent devilfish dwelling in the deepest ocean trenches persist, although if these rumors are true, these deep-dwelling devilfish do not often come to the surface.

DEVILFISH

Large monstrosity, neutral evil

Armor Class 15 (natural armor)

Hit Points 133 (14d10+56)

Speed 10 ft., swim 40 ft.

STR	DEX	CON	INT	WIS	CHA
17 (+3)	17 (+3)	18 (+4)	3 (–4)	14 (+2)	8 (–1)

Saving Throws Con +7, Int -1, Wis +5

Skills Athletics +6, Stealth +6

Senses darkvision 120 ft., passive Perception 12

Languages Abyssal, Aquan, Common

Challenge 5 (1,800 XP)

Water Dependency. The devilfish can only breathe underwater but can hold its breath out of water for 4 hours.

ACTIONS

Multiattack. The devilfish makes one bite attack and two tentacle attacks.

Bite. Melee Weapon Attack. +6 to hit, 15 ft. reach, one target. *Hit:* 7 (1d8 + 3) piercing damage plus 14 (4d6) poison damage. If the target is a creature, it must succeed a DC 15 Constitution saving throw or become poisoned. A poisoned creature can attempt another saving throw at the end of each of its turns.

Tentacle. Melee Weapon Attack. +6 to hit, 15 ft. reach, one target. *Hit:* 7 (1d8 + 3) bludgeoning damage. Instead of dealing damage, the devilfish can grapple the target (escape DC 15).

Jet Away (1/Day). The devilfish can suddenly move 240 feet away in a straight line, provoking opportunity attacks.

REACTIONS

Nautilus Defense. When attacked, a devilfish can harden its supple skin into a rigid nautiloid shell. This increases its AC to 17 but reduces its swim speed to 30 ft. and reduces the distance it can Jet Away to 120 feet. It can discard this shell at any time as a bonus action, but it cannot form a new shell until it has completed a long rest. The shell itself crumbles to sandy grit after 1 minute.

DRAKE, SEA

While obviously the product of draconic inbreeding, the heritage of sea drakes is less clear than that of other lesser dragons like wyverns and the like. Though among the strongest of such "false dragons," sea drakes lack the mental acuity of their true dragon forebears, though they do possess a certain brutal cunning. Although amphibious, sea drakes spend the majority of their time in shallow coastal waters. Sea drakes are up to 14 feet long from their noses to the tips of their powerful tails. They weigh 2,000 pounds.

Rampage. The most solitary of all drakes, sea drakes prefer to hunt alone. Occasionally, however, they band together in packs to hunt larger prey. Such rampages can be a significant danger to coastal shipping.

Sea Drake

Large dragon, neutral evil

Armor Class 15 (natural armor)

Hit Points 152 (16d10+64)

Speed 30 ft., fly 60 ft., swim 60 ft.

STR	DEX	CON	INT	WIS	CHA
23 (+6)	15 (+2)	18 (+4)	8 (−1)	10 (+0)	9 (−1)

Saving Throws Con +7, Str +9

Skills Athletics +9, Intimidation +5

Damage Immunities lightning

Senses darkvision 60 ft., passive Perception 10

Languages Draconic

Challenge 6 (2,300 XP)

Amphibious. The sea drake can breathe air and water.

Siege Monster. The sea drake deals double damage to objects and structures.

Actions

Multiattack. The sea drake makes one bite attack and one tail attack.

Bite. Melee Weapon Attack. +9 to hit, reach 10 ft., one target. *Hit:* 22 (3d10 + 6) piercing damage.

Tail. Melee Weapon Attack. +9 to hit, reach 10 ft., one target. *Hit:* 17 (3d8 + 6) bludgeoning damage.

Ball Lightning Breath (Recharges 5–6). The sea drake can breathe a ball of chain lightning as per the *chain lightning* spell except that each creature struck must succeed a DC 15 Dexterity saving throw or take 3d6 lightning damage. If it wishes, it can exhale tiny drifting motes of crackling electricity that deal no damage but rather act as *dancing lights.*

Capsize. The sea drake is skilled at ramming its bulk into the side of watercraft up to 20 feet long and 10 feet wide, whether swooping from above or swimming up from below. As an action, it can make a Strength (Athletics) check against every creature on board the boat, seeking to knock creatures prone or knock them overboard. It makes a single check and compares the result to all creatures on board. At the GM's option, if it successfully Shoves all creatures on board, the entire boat capsizes.

Reactions

Draconic Surge (3/day). The sea drake can take an additional Dash action on its turn.

DRAUGR

Draugr smell of decay and the sea, and drip water wherever they go. These barnacle-encrusted walking corpses look like zombies, but with a fell light in their eyes and dripping with rank water that gives off a nauseating stench. These foul beings are usually created when humanoid creatures are lost at sea in regions haunted by evil spirits or necromantic effects. The corpses of these drowned sailors cling fiercely to unlife, attacking any living creatures that intrude upon them. Their attacks smear rancid flesh, rotting seaweed, and swaths of vermin on whatever they hit.

Grim Crew. In the case of draugr who manifest when an entire ship sinks, these undead usually stay with the wreck of their ship. Some draugr may be found under the control of aquatic necromancers, while others may wander the seas as undead pirates aboard ghost ships.

Lifeless. As animated corpses, draugr do not eat, sleep, or breathe.

DRAUGR

Medium undead, chaotic evil

Armor Class 12 (studded leather)

Hit Points 19 (3d8+6)

Speed 30 ft., swim 30 ft.

STR	DEX	CON	INT	WIS	CHA
15 (+2)	10 (+0)	15 (+2)	8 (-1)	10 (+0)	13 (+1)

Skills Athletics +4, Perception +2, Stealth +2

Damage Immunities poison

Damage Resistances fire

Condition Immunities exhaustion, poisoned

Senses darkvision 60 ft.; passive Perception 12

Languages understands the languages it knew in life but can't speak

Challenge 1/4 (50 XP)

ACTIONS

Greataxe. Melee Weapon Attack: +4 to hit, reach 5 ft., one target. *Hit:* 8 (1d12 + 2) slashing damage, and once per round on the draugr's turn the target must make a DC 11 Constitution saving throw. On a failure, the target is incapacitated until the beginning off the draugr's next turn. Creatures that are immune to being poisoned are not incapacitated.

DRAUGR CAPTAIN

Medium undead, chaotic evil

Armor Class 13 (studded leather)

Hit Points 90 (12d8+36)

Speed 30 ft., swim 30 ft.

STR	DEX	CON	INT	WIS	CHA
17 (+3)	12 (+1)	17 (+3)	10 (+0)	12 (+1)	15 (+2)

Skills Athletics +5, Perception +3, Stealth +3

Damage Immunities poison

Damage Resistances fire

Condition Immunities exhaustion, poisoned

Senses darkvision 60 ft.; passive Perception 13

Languages understands the languages it knew in life but can't speak

Challenge 2 (450 XP)

ACTIONS

Multiattack. The draugr captain makes two greataxe attacks.

Greataxe. Melee Weapon Attack: +5 to hit, reach 5 ft., one target. *Hit:* 9 (1d12 + 3) slashing damage, and once per round on the draugr captain's turn, the target must succeed on a DC 13 Constitution saving throw or its hit point maximum is reduced by 5. This reduction lasts until the target finishes a long rest. The target dies if this effect reduces its hit point maximum to 0. A humanoid slain by this attack rises 24 hours later as a draugr under the draugr captain's control, unless the humanoid is restored to life or its body is destroyed. The draugr captain can have no more than twelve draugr under its control at one time.

Mist (3/Day). The daugr captain creates a 20-foot-radius sphere of fog centered on its space. The sphere spreads around corners, and its area is lightly obscured. Anything more than 5 feet away through the fog is heavily obscured. It lasts for 5 minutes or until a wind of moderate or greater speed (at least 10 miles per hour) disperses it.

DRAUGR CREW

Huge swarm of Medium undead, chaotic evil

Armor Class 17 (half plate armor)

Hit Points 247 (26d12+78)

Speed 30 ft., swim 30 ft.

STR	DEX	CON	INT	WIS	CHA
21 (+6)	18 (+4)	16 (+3)	12 (+1)	14 (+2)	17 (+3)

Saving Throws Dex +8, Str +10

Damage Immunities poison

Damage Resistance fire

Condition Immunities charmed, exhaustion, frightened, grappled, paralyzed, petrified, prone, restrained, stunned

Skills Athletics +14, Stealth +8

Senses darkvision 60 ft., passive Perception 12

Languages Common

Challenge 12 (8,400 XP)

Innate Spellcasting. A draugr crew's spellcasting ability is Charisma (spell save DC 15). It can innately cast the following spells, requiring no material components:

3/day: *charm person, fog cloud*

Part of the Ship, Part of the Crew. Any humanoid killed by the draugr crew rises as a draugr 1d4 rounds later, healing the draugr crew by a number of hit points equal to twice the humanoid's Hit Dice.

Swarm. The draugr crew can occupy another creature's space and vice versa, and the crew can move through any opening large enough for a Medium draugr. The draugr crew can't regain hit points except through its Part of the Ship, Part of the Crew trait.

ACTIONS

Volley of Blows. Melee Weapon Attack. +10 to hit, reach 0 ft., four creatures in the draugr crew's space. *Hit:* 19 (2d12 + 6) slashing damage, or 12 (1d12+6) damage if the draugr crew has less than half of its hit points. Any creatures damaged by the draugr crew must succeed a DC 17 Constitution saving throw. On a failure, the creature is incapacitated until the beginning off the draugr crew's next turn. Creatures that are immune to being poisoned are not incapacitated.

Pressgang (1/day). The draugr crew can cast *dominate person* on one creature that is already charmed by the crew, requiring a DC 15 Wisdom saving throw made with disadvantage to negate the effect.

CREATING A DRAUGR NPC

To turn an existing NPC into a draugr, apply the following changes:

- +2 Str, -2 Int
- Darkvision 60 ft.
- Swim 30 ft.
- Resistance to fire damage
- Immune to poison damage
- Immune to being poisoned and exhaustion
- Understands the languages it knew in life but can't speak
- Once per round on its turn, when it hits with a melee attack, it may incapacitate a target (see above) with a DC of 8 + proficiency bonus + Charisma modifier.

This alters the NPC's Challenge.

DUPPY

A duppy is the spirit of a cruel and brutal sailor who died by violence on land, away from his ship and crew, and thus was unable to receive a proper burial at sea.

Hounded in Death. While its ghostly form is evidence enough of its twisted hatred, a duppy also possesses power over a pack of faithful, otherworldly hounds that share in their master's malevolence. The appearance of a duppy is often preceded by the distant sound of unearthly howling.

Duppies typically seek out sailors and pirates when exacting their vengeance, inflicting great violence on those living creatures who remind them of what they lost. For this reason, duppies are most often found in seaside towns or nearby beaches, and settlements that rely on the ocean know to fear and hate these spectral beings.

Dead Man's Chest. Some tales claim that duppies arise near the treasures they buried while they were still alive, and ambitious sailors who buy into these stories might attempt to capture a duppy. However, few creatures can muster powers strong enough to cage a duppy, whose hounds confound enemies and allow the ghostly monster to attack victims from all sides. Those who do manage to trick a duppy into a magical trap are wise to keep the horror confined until the daytime, when its otherworldly abilities are hindered and it can be more easily defeated.

DUPPY

Medium undead, chaotic evil

Armor Class 15 (natural armor)

Hit Points 84 (13d8+26)

Speed fly 40 ft.

STR	DEX	CON	INT	WIS	CHA
10 (+0)	22 (+6)	14 (+2)	13 (+1)	15 (+2)	19 (+4)

Saving Throws Dex +9, Cha +7

Skills Intimidation +10, Stealth +12

Damage Resistance acid, cold, fire, lightning, thunder; bludgeoning, piercing, and slashing from nonmagical attacks

Damage Immunities necrotic, poison

Damage Vulnerabilities radiant

Senses darkvision 60 ft., passive Perception 12

Languages Common

Challenge 7 (2,900 XP)

Innate Spellcasting. A duppy's spellcasting ability is Charisma (spell save DC 15). It can innately cast the following spells, requiring no material components:

1/day each: *faithful hound* (+8 to hit), *invisibility*

Sunlight Weakness. While in sunlight, the duppy has disadvantage on attack rolls, ability checks, and saving throws.

ACTIONS

Strength Drain. *Melee Weapon Attack.* +9 to hit, 5 ft. reach, one target. *Hit:* 45 (7d12) necrotic damage. The target's Strength score is reduced by 1d4. The target dies if this reduces its Strength to 0. Otherwise, the reduction lasts until the target finishes a short or long rest.

EEL, ELECTRIC

This six-foot-long, snake-like fish moves slowly. A strange popping and snapping sound occasionally emits from the creature's body. The electric eel is a curious fish that breathes air instead of water, yet certainly its most unusual characteristic is its ability to generate powerful jolts of electricity.

ELECTRIC EEL

Small beast, unaligned

Armor Class 12

Hit Points 13 (2d6+6)

Speed 5 ft., swim 30 ft.

STR	DEX	CON	INT	WIS	CHA
13 (+1)	14 (+2)	16 (+3)	1 (-5)	10 (+0)	4 (-3)

Damage Resistances lightning

Skills Perception +2, Stealth +4

Senses blindsight 60 ft.; passive Perception 12

Languages -

Challenge 1/4 (50 XP)

Hold Breath. The electric eel can hold its breath for 10 minutes.

ACTIONS

Bite. *Melee Weapon Attack:* +4 to hit, reach 5 ft., one target. *Hit:* 5 (1d6+2) piercing damage.

Tail. *Melee Weapon Attack:* +4 to hit, reach 5 ft., one target. *Hit:* 5 (1d6+2) lightning damage. On a critical hit, the target must succeed on a DC 13 Constitution saving throw or be stunned. At the end of each of its turns, the target can make a new saving throw; on a success, it is no longer stunned.

EEL, GIANT MORAY

This sixteen-foot-long eel slithers through the water with uncanny grace, mouth open to display large teeth and a second set of jaws. Giant moray eels are warm-water animals that lie in wait to ambush prey. Once they get hold of prey, or an intruder, they are tenacious biters, gnawing and tearing flesh.

GIANT MORAY EEL

Large beast, unaligned

Armor Class 15 (natural armor)

Hit Points 52 (7d10+14)

Speed 0 ft., swim 30 ft.

STR	DEX	CON	INT	WIS	CHA
18 (+4)	14 (+2)	15 (+2)	1 (-5)	12 (+1)	4 (-3)

Skills Perception +3, Stealth +4

Senses blindsight 60 ft.; passive Perception 13

Languages -

Challenge 2 (450 XP)

Water Breathing. The giant moray eel can breathe only underwater.

ACTIONS

Bite. *Melee Weapon Attack:* +6 to hit, reach 10 ft., one target. *Hit:* 11 (2d6+4) piercing damage, and the target is grappled (escape DC 16). Until this grapple ends, the creature is restrained, and the giant moray eel can't grapple another target.

ELEMENTAL, OCEAN

Ocean elementals are patient, relentless creatures made of living fresh or salt water. They prefer to hide or drag their opponents into the water to gain an advantage. As with other elementals, all ocean elementals have their own unique shapes and appearances. Some appear as wave-like creatures with vaguely humanoid faces and smaller wave "arms" to either side, but many adopt the shape of an aquatic creature, such as a shark or octopus, but made entirely out of water.

Mythic Power. An ocean elemental is infused with legendary power, a manifestation of the power of gods of nature and the elements, or an elder colossus formed of the primal energies and raw matter of creation that has endured through all the ages. These divinely anointed creatures have maximum hit points for their hit dice to represent their staying power and danger.

OCEAN ELEMENTAL

Huge elemental, neutral

Armor Class 16 (natural armor)

Hit Points 320 (20d12 + 80)

Speed 30 ft., swim 90 ft.

STR	DEX	CON	INT	WIS	CHA
18 (+4)	14 (+2)	18 (+4)	5 (-3)	10 (+0)	8 (-1)

Damage Resistances acid; bludgeoning, piercing, and slashing from nonmagical attacks

Damage Immunities poison

Condition Immunities exhaustion, grappled, paralyzed, petrified, poisoned, prone, restrained, unconscious

Senses darkvision 60 ft., passive Perception 10

Languages Aquan

Challenge 19 (22,000 XP)

Drench. The elemental's touch puts out non-magical flames of Large size or smaller. The creature can dispel magical fire it touches as dispel magic.

Freeze. If the elemental takes cold damage, it partially freezes; its speed is reduced by 20 feet until the end of its next turn.

Water Form. The elemental can enter a hostile creature's space and stop there. It can move through a space as narrow as 1 inch wide without squeezing.

Water Mastery. An ocean elemental gains a +2 bonus on attack and damage rolls if both it and its opponent are touching water. If the opponent or the elemental is touching the ground, the elemental takes a −2 penalty on attack and damage rolls.

ACTIONS

Multiattack. The elemental uses vortex (either to start or dismiss the whirlpool) then makes three slam attacks.

Slam. Melee Weapon Attack. +10 to hit, reach 10 ft., one target. *Hit:* 22 (4d8 + 4) bludgeoning damage.

Vortex. An ocean elemental can create a whirlpool centered on itself in a 20-foot sphere. Creatures smaller than the elemental take 13 (2d8 + 4) bludgeoning damage when caught in the whirlpool and are pulled off their feet in to the swirling water if they fail a DC 18 Dexterity saving throw. Creatures already caught in the vortex at the start of their turn automatically take 13 (2d8 + 4) bludgeoning damage and may attempt another saving throw as an action to free themselves. Creatures with a swim speed have advantage on this saving throw.

Creatures trapped in the vortex cannot move except to go where the elemental carries them or to escape the vortex. They have disadvantage on attack rolls and the ocean elemental has advantage on attack rolls against them, but they can otherwise act normally. However, trapped creatures must make a DC 18 Constitution saving throw to cast spells; if the save fails, the spell is lost without effect. Creatures able to breathe water save only when casting spells with somatics.

The elemental can eject any swept-up creatures whenever it wishes as a bonus action, depositing them in its space. The vortex can only form underwater and cannot move beyond the body of water.

If the ocean elemental is within 10 feet of the surface when it creates a vortex, it may choose to blanket the surface of the water with dense fog and spray, as the *fog cloud* spell.

Whelm (Recharge 4-6). Each creature in the elemental's space must succeed on a DC 18 Strength saving throw. On a failure, a target takes 22 (4d8 + 4) bludgeoning damage. If it is Large or smaller, it is also grappled (escape DC 18). Until this grapple ends, the target is restrained and unable to breathe unless it can breathe water. If the saving throw is successful, the target is pushed out of the elemental's space. The elemental can grapple one huge creature or up to two large or smaller creatures at one time. At the start of each of the elemental's turns, each target grappled by it takes 22 (4d8 + 4) bludgeoning damage. A creature within 5 feet of the elemental can pull out a creature or object out of it by taking an action to make a DC 18 Strength and succeeding.

FISH, BLADEFISH

A school of human-sized grey fish moves as one. Their long flat bills and rigid fins are bordered in razor-thin silver scales.

Scintillating Wave. Fast and strong, bladefish swim through the warm currents of deep ocean waters in instinctive circuits that cover thousands of miles. These cycles take them through their entire life cycle, including live birth, adolescence, hunting, and mating, though beautiful to behold, bladefish are deadly carnivores and deliver brutal blows very rapidly as they charge in, swim past, and charge in again. Their skulls narrow to a flat, horizontal blade and their tail fins sport a similar vertical protrusion. Both bear shining scales along these sharp edges as decoration. A long, sharp mouth blade is ideal for hunting and defense, while the brightest sheen along its blades attracts the most desirable mates.

Storm of Blades. The greatest weapon bladefish have is in their numbers. Vast storms of them swim their lifelong circuits near the water's surface and as deep as 200 feet. When one senses an intruder, it determines whether the threat is manageable or overwhelming and reacts by charging or fleeing, respectively. The entire community of bladefish joins in that reaction, swimming away as one or attacking in a rapid frenzy of sharp bills. Weaker bladefish are left behind or join the fight late and risk losing their meal to more aggressive members.

An adult bladefish is 7 feet long and weighs 600 pounds. Larger, rarer species can reach 40 feet in length and live for over a hundred years.

BLADEFISH

Medium beast, unaligned

Armor Class 14 (natural armor)

Hit Points 104 (11d8 + 55)

Speed 0 ft., swim 60 ft.

STR	DEX	CON	INT	WIS	CHA
23 (+6)	12 (+1)	21 (+5)	1 (-5)	12 (+1)	5 (-3)

Skills Perception +4

Senses blindsight 10 ft., passive Perception 14

Languages —

Challenge 5 (1,800 XP)

Pack Tactics. The bladefish has advantage on attack rolls against a creature if at least one of the bladefish's allies is within 5 feet of the creature and the ally isn't incapacitated.

Razor Fin. A bladefish has quick reflexes and powerful muscles along its length. If it strikes the same target with its blade and tail slap attacks it does an additonal 10 necrotic damage as the target bleeds from the gashes made by the bladefish.

Swim-By Attack. A bladefish is perfectly suited for attacking on the move. It does not provoke attacks of opportunity so long as it has attacked in the same turn it has provoked.

Water Breathing. The bladefish can breathe only underwater.

ACTIONS

Multiattack. The bladefish makes one blade and one tail slap attack so long as it has moved at least 5-feet before making the first attack roll.

Blade. Melee Weapon Attack: +9 to hit, reach 5 ft., one target. *Hit:* 17 (2d10 + 6) piercing damage. This attack scores a critical hit on a natural 19 or 20.

Tail Slap. Melee Weapon Attack: +9 to hit, reach 5 ft., one target. *Hit:* 11 (1d10 + 6) slashing damage. This attack scores a critical hit on a natural 19 or 20.

FISH, DINICHTHYS

This horrific fish has a powerful grey body, with a head of hard white plates. Its wide mouth more resembles curved blades of bloodstained bone.

Primordial Punisher. Among the deadlier animals of the sea, the mighty dinichthys holds its own against dragons and magical beasts. Its punishing bite allows it to both defend itself and feed from the sea's hardiest animals. Dinichthyses hunt at any depth greater than 20 feet, chasing prey for miles in any direction before resuming a natural migration toward decennial mating waters.

Neverfull. Dinichthyses are voracious, often biting a chunk of flesh out of a sizable creature so it can follow the bleeding quarry to any social unit it might flee to for protection.

Dinichthyses live for approximately 100 years. An adult is 30 feet long and weighs 22,000 pounds.

FISH, DINICHTHYS

Huge beast, unaligned

Armor Class 14 (natural armor)

Hit Points 253 (22d10+132)

Speed 0 ft., swim 50 ft.

STR	DEX	CON	INT	WIS	CHA
20 (+5)	12 (+1)	23 (+6)	3 (-4)	12 (+1)	7 (-2)

Skills Perception +5

Senses blindsight 120 ft., passive Perception 15

Languages —

Challenge 12 (8,400 XP)

Swim-By Attack. A dinichthys is perfectly suited for attacking on the move. A dinichthys that uses its action to attack does not provoke opportunity attacks for the rest of its turn.

Vicious Bite. The dinichthys scores critical hits on natural rolls of 15 to 20. In addition, its critical hit damage is always maximized doing 35 piercing damage and inflicting an additional 7 (2d6) necrotic damage from bleeding. This bleeding can only be stopped with a DC 15 Wisdom (Medicine) check or through any magical healing. This damage is cumulative. For example, a creature who has been hit by two critical hits from a dinichthys vicious bite suffers 14 (4d6) necrotic damage per round.

Water Breathing. The dinichthys can breathe only underwater.

ACTIONS

Multiattack. The dinichthys makes two bite attacks.

Bite. *Melee Weapon Attack:* +9 to hit, reach 5 ft., one target. *Hit:* 22 (5d6 + 5) piercing damage.

GIANT, OCEAN

Ocean giants embody the great extremes of the sea. Their skin colors vary from deep blue to pale green, and their eyes and hair range from foamy white to coral pink. They decorate themselves with the treasures of the sea, wearing shell jewelry or scrimshaw, and clothing woven from underwater plants, or even salvaged sails. Adult ocean giants stand approximately 22 feet tall and weigh about 15,000 pounds. Most live to be about 500 years old.

Musical Conches. Each ocean giant carries a hand-crafted musical horn made from a conch shell, an object of cultural significance representing its family history and travels on the vast sea.

Ocean Rulers. Many ocean giants view themselves as guardians of the sea, its creatures, and those who travel the waves, safeguarding their charges from remarkable coral towers. Others, however, claim domains measuring thousands of leagues, enslaving the beasts and aquatic races within and shattering any ship that dares trespass near their citadels of urchins and bones.

Ocean Giant

Huge giant, chaotic neutral

Armor Class 18 (natural armor)

Hit Points 262 (21d12+126)

Speed 50 ft., swim 40 ft.

STR	DEX	CON	INT	WIS	CHA
29 (+9)	11 (+0)	22 (+6)	12 (+1)	14 (+2)	18 (+4)

Saving Throws Str +14, Con +11, Wis +7, Cha +9

Skills Nature +6, Perception +7, Performance +14

Damage Resistances cold, lightning

Senses darkvision 60 ft., passive Perception 17

Languages Aquan, Common, Giant

Challenge 13 (10,000 XP)

Amphibious. An ocean giant can breathe air and water.

Innate Spellcasting. The giant's innate spellcasting ability is Charisma (spell save DC 17). It can innately cast the following spells, requiring no material components:

3/day each: *control water, gust of wind, water breathing*

1/day: *control weather*

Powerful Trident. Ocean giants are masters of the trident, a weapon well-suited for underwater combat. A trident deals one extra die of its damage when the ocean giant hits with it (included in the attack).

Actions

Multiattack. The giant makes two trident attacks.

Trident. Melee or Ranged Weapon Attack: +14 to hit, reach 10 ft. or range 20/60 ft., one target. *Hit:* 23 (4d6 + 9) piercing damage, or 27 (4d8 + 9) piercing damage if used with two hands to make a melee attack. If the ocean giant scores a critical hit, it rolls damage dice three times, instead of twice.

Rock. Ranged Weapon Attack: +14 to hit, range 60/240 ft., one target. *Hit:* 35 (4d12 + 9) bludgeoning damage.

Conch (Recharge 5-6). The giant blasts its conch. All creatures in a 60-foot cone must make a DC 17 Constitution saving throw. A creature takes 58 (13d8) thunder damage on a failed save, or half as much damage on a successful one. A target that fails its saving throw is stunned for 1 round and deafened for 1 minute. At the end of each of its turns, a target can attempt a new saving throw; on a success, the target is no longer deafened.

GLOBSTER

A globster is a living collection of half-digested parts from large sea creatures such as whales and squid. Passersby usually discover it by smell long before they see it. Many unfortunate folk who happen upon a globster mistake it for the carcass of a beached sea animal, getting too close before discovering the seemingly dead creature is very much alive. For a time, sages believed globsters were undead—that they were simply undulating wads of rotting flesh animated with a drive to feed. However, globsters are actually living creatures.

Globsters usually wash up on a beach or float to the shore to feed on terrestrial stock for a few hours before returning to the safety of water. Some say the tides and phases of the moon are to blame for the times globsters come to land to feed. Globsters reproduce by mixing parts of their own foul bodies with the poorly digested remains of their meals.

ACTIONS

Pseudopod. *Melee Weapon Attack:* +8 to hit, 5 ft. reach, 1 target. *Hit:* 12 (2d6 + 5) bludgeoning damage. Any creature struck by this attack must make a DC 15 Constitution saving throw or be poisoned for 1d4 rounds.

Nauseating Grasp. When a globster successfully grapples a Medium or smaller creature, the target takes damage and may be poisoned as if the globster had hit with its pseudopod attack, and it can move at full speed while carrying the grappled creature.

GLOBSTER

Large ooze, unaligned

Armor Class 15 (natural armor)

Hit Points 95 (10d10+40)

Speed 20 ft., swim 40 ft.

STR	DEX	CON	INT	WIS	CHA
20 (+5)	1 (-5)	18 (+4)	1 (-5)	1 (-5)	1 (-5)

Skills Athletics +8

Damage Resistance thunder, bludgeoning

Damage Immunities acid, piercing

Condition Immunities blinded, charmed, deafened, exhaustion, frightened, prone

Senses blindsight 60 ft., passive Perception 5

Languages —

Challenge 5 (1800 XP)

Create Spawn (1/Day). The globster takes 3 (1d6) damage and creates a new globster which attacks the nearest non-globster creature. This ability can only be used if the globster is well-fed (eating at least 4 Medium creatures or 1 Large since it last spawned, or the equivalent).

Stench. Any living creature within 30 feet of a globster at the beginning of its turn must make a DC 13 Constitution saving throw or be poisoned until the beginning of its next turn. If the globster is killed, this stench persists on its corpse for 1d10 days.

GOLEM, CANNON

A cannon golem is a technomagical construct enchanted into a massive heap of jagged metal in a humanoid form, its enormous cannon tracking movement with mechanical precision. A cannon golem's internal workings are a mechanical labyrinth; its extradimensional pockets constantly process new black powder to fire its arcane weapon. A cannon golem stands 12 feet tall and weighs around 8,000 pounds.

CANNON GOLEM

Large construct, unaligned

Armor Class 20 (natural armor)

Hit Points 210 (20d10 + 100)

Speed 30 ft.

STR	DEX	CON	INT	WIS	CHA
24 (+7)	9 (-1)	20 (+5)	3 (-4)	11 (+0)	1 (-5)

Damage Immunities fire, poison, psychic; bludgeoning, piercing, and slashing from nonmagical attacks that aren't adamantine

Condition Immunities charmed, exhaustion, frightened, paralyzed, petrified, poisoned

Senses darkvision 120 ft., passive Perception 10

Languages understands the languages of its creator but can't speak

Challenge 16 (15,000 XP)

Fire Absorption. Whenever the golem is subjected to fire damage, it takes no damage and instead regains a number of hit points equal to the fire damage dealt. However, if it fails its saving throw against a fire spell that deals at least 20 points of damage, it must make a Constitution saving throw against the same DC. If this save fails, its cannon immediately backfires, dealing 6d6 bludgeoning damage to the golem (this bypasses its damage immunity).

Immutable Form. The golem is immune to any spell or effect that would alter its form.

Magic Resistance. The golem has advantage on saving throws against spells and other magical effects.

Magic Weapons. The golem's weapon attacks are magical.

ACTIONS

Mutliattack. A cannon golem has a magical cannon built into one arm rather than wielding a sword. It makes two melee fist attacks or one fist attack and one cannon attack.

Fist. *Melee Weapon Attack:* +12 to hit, reach 5 ft., one target. *Hit:* 20 (3d8 + 7) bludgeoning damage.

Cannon. *Ranged Weapon Attack:* +12 to hit, range 80/320 ft., one target. *Hit:* 33 (4d12 + 7) bludgeoning damage. When a cannon golem hits a target with its cannon, it can make a Strength (Athletics) check as a bonus action to shove that target, pushing it away and knocking it prone on a successful check. It has advantage on this check if the target is Medium or smaller.

Cannonade (Recharge 6). The golem shoots a cannon blast that fills a 60-foot line or a 15-foot cone. Each creature in that area must make a DC 19 Dexterity saving throw, taking 45 (10d8) bludgeoning damage on a failed save, or half as much on a successful one.

REACTIONS

Cannon Punch (1/Turn). When a cannon golem scores a critical hit with its slam attack, as a bonus action it can make a cannon attack against the same target. It cannot use this ability if it already has made a ranged cannon attack or cannonade on the same turn.

GOLEM, CORAL

Coral golems are constructs made entirely of colonies of living coral drawn from the ocean. While their sharpened appendages are capable of performing tasks that require meticulous precision, they are equally useful in martial combat. Wizards and sorcerers employ coral golems to collect delicate specimens of plant life from local beaches, spear and retrieve fish from the ocean for meals, and protect valuable locations such as their masters' homes or veins of minerals and other potent resources. A coral golem is 9 feet tall and weighs 1,000 pounds.

CORAL GOLEM

Large construct, unaligned

Armor Class 15 (natural armor)

Hit Points 119 (14d10+42)

Speed 30 ft.

STR	DEX	CON	INT	WIS	CHA
20 (+5)	11 (+0)	16 (+3)	3 (-4)	11 (+0)	1 (-5)

Damage Immunities poison, psychic; bludgeoning, piercing, and slashing from nonmagical attacks that aren't adamantine

Condition Immunities charmed, exhaustion, frightened, paralyzed, petrified, poisoned

Senses darkvision 120 ft.; passive Perception 10

Languages understands the languages of its creator but can't speak

Challenge 9 (5,000 XP)

Aquatic Reconstruction. The golem regains 10 hit points at the start of its turn if it has at least 1 hit point and it is touching a body of saltwater of a size equal to or greater than its own body.

Immutable Form. The golem is immune to any spell or effect that would alter its form.

Magic Resistance. The golem has advantage on saving throws against spells and other magical effects.

Magic Weapons. The golem's weapon attacks are magical.

ACTIONS

Multiattack. The golem makes two claw attacks.

Claw. *Melee Weapon Attack:* +9 to hit, reach 5 ft., one target. *Hit:* 15 (3d6 + 5) slashing damage. If the golem scores a critical hit, it rolls damage dice three times, instead of twice.

HAG, REEF

Monstrous sea witches, these wicked hags possess terrifying features that few dare look upon, though their powers of illusion allow them to disguise themselves as alluring mermaids or sirens. Reveling in discord, the foul creatures drag sailors to watery graves and torment the peoples of the oceans with wicked promises, turning them into savage servants under the sea. Sea hags are always terrible to look upon, and despite their gluttonous ways, they are usually emaciated creatures who look half-starved. Most stand about 6 feet tall and weigh 150 pounds.

Storm Hag Covens. Reef hags form covens similar to other hags, almost always with a pair of lesser sea hags. Those living near coastal areas may join forces with a saltmarsh-dwelling green hag, though the arrogant green hags often vie for dominance and mixed covens may break down in bloody murder. A coven with a reef hag as a member has access to the following additional spells: *conjure minor elementals* (water only), *hallucinatory terrain*, *water breathing*, and *water walk*.

Toxic Tolerance. Reef hags cultivate gardens of venomous sea life and crustaceans around their lairs like living traps for the unwary. Toxic urchins, anemones, corals, eels, spinefish, and more await any who would dare face her in her lair beneath the coral.

Reef Hag

Medium fey, chaotic evil

Armor Class 14 (natural armor)

Hit Points 145 (17d10+68)

Speed 30 ft., swim 40 ft.

STR	DEX	CON	INT	WIS	CHA
20 (+5)	16 (+3)	18 (+4)	12 (+1)	12 (+1)	13 (+1)

Damage Immunities poison

Condition Immunities poisoned

Senses darkvision 60 ft., fog sense, passive Perception 11

Languages Aquan, Common, Sylvan

Challenge 5 (2,900 XP)

Horrific Appearance. The sight of a reef hag is so revolting that anyone within 30 feet (other than another hag) and can see what the hag truly looks like must succeed on a DC 15 Wisdom saving throw or be frightened for 1 minute. A creature may make a new saving throw at the end of each turn, ending the effect on a success. If the saving throw succeeds the creature becomes immune to this effect for 24 hours. A creature may avert their eyes from the reef hag unless they are surprised by the form. A creature gains disadvantage on attack rolls against the hag until the start of their next turn if they avert their eyes.

Illusory Appearance. The reef hag can make herself appear as a medium female humanoid. Creatures that touch the reef hag or make a successful DC 16 Intelligence (Investigation) check can successfully see through the disguise.

Reef Mistress. Reef hags can converse with ordinary sea life, including plants and animals, as if they had continuous *speak with animals* and *speak with plants*. As an action, they can cause such sea life within 30 feet to impede other creatures, acting as difficult terrain, or can cause difficult terrain caused by seaweed and small sea life to clear and become as ordinary terrain. She can exclude any creatures she wishes from difficult terrain she creates with this ability, and she herself is never impeded by it.

Actions

Multiattack. The reef hag can make two claw attacks or two harpoon attacks.

Claws. Melee Weapon Attack: +8 to hit, 5 ft. reach, 1 target. *Hit:* 13 (2d6+5) slashing damage. If the reef hag hits a Medium or smaller with both claw attacks, they are grappled (DC 15 to escape) and restrained until the grapple ends.

Harpoon. Melee Weapon Attack: +8 to hit, 10 ft. reach, 1 target. *Hit:* 14 (2d8 + 5) piercing damage.

Salt Wife's Glare. The reef hag can target a single creature that is within 30 feet and frightened of her. They must pass a DC 15 Wisdom saving throw against this magical effect or be reduced to 0 HP. A creature affected by this ability becomes doesn't make death saving throws and gains the ability to breathe underwater. While underwater the creature cannot regain HP. After spending a day submerged in salt water, the creature must succeed at a DC 10 Constitution save or be transformed into a merrow[SRD] and regain their HP. If transformed into a merrow they regard the reef hag as their beloved mistress. She gains advantage on Charisma (Deception) checks when interacting with the merrow she transforms, and they in turn become immune to her horrific appearance. This transformation cannot be dispelled but can be reversed with *remove curse*. This effect becomes permanent after seven days have passed.

HAG, STORM

A storm hag's wrinkled face contains a look of gleeful distaste, and her eyes are thick with cataracts, rendering her gaze pupil-less. A storm hag's hair is wild and unruly with static electricity popping and crackling throughout the mass. Her mouth hangs open, revealing thin pointed teeth with small arcs of electricity jumping across them. Black talons sprout from her fingertips, likewise crackling with electricity. A storm hag weighs 70 pounds and stands around 4 feet tall, though if she stood up straight, she could easily reach 5 feet.

Storm Hag Covens. When the clouds turn gray and the winds pick up into a howl, wise travelers pray that the cause is only a natural tempest and the foul weather is not connected with a storm hag and a group of hags working with her. Storm hags are hateful creatures, and strangely, their hate is one of the few things that brings them pleasure. A storm hag is haughty and views her way of doing things as the only proper approach, forcing coven members to ride a fine line between flattery and submission. A coven with a storm hag as a member has access to the following additional spells: *call lightning, control weather, water breathing,* and *wind walk.*

STORM HAG

Medium fey, chaotic evil

Armor Class 19 (natural armor)

Hit Points 231 (22d8+132)

Speed 30 ft., 60 ft. fly

STR	DEX	CON	INT	WIS	CHA
18 (+4)	20 (+5)	22 (+6)	17 (+3)	19 (+4)	22 (+6)

Damage Immunities lightning, thunder

Senses darkvision 60 ft., passive Perception 14

Languages Common, Giant

Challenge 12 (8,400 XP)

Innate Spellcasting. A storm hag's spellcasting ability is Charisma (spell save DC 18). It can innately cast the following spells, requiring no material components:

At will: *gust of wind*

3/Day: *call lightning, sleet storm*

1/Day: *lightning bolt, wind wall*

Storm Rider. A storm hag is immune to wind effects and cannot be damaged or forced to move by wind of any strength.

ACTIONS

Multiattack. A storm hag makes 2 claw attacks and 1 bite attack.

Claw. Melee Weapon Attack: +8 to hit, 5 ft. reach, 1 target. *Hit:* 14 (3d6 + 4) slashing damage. Any creature struck by this and wearing predominantly metal armor or weaponry takes an additional 3 (1d6) lightning damage.

Bite. Melee Weapon Attack: +8 to hit, 5 ft. reach, 1 target. *Hit:* 17 (3d8 + 4) piercing damage.

REACTIONS

Whipping Winds. When a creature moves into a square within 15 feet of a storm hag, as a reaction she can force that creature to make a DC 14 Strength saving throw or be knocked prone or pushed 10 feet in a direction of her choosing (including moving the creature adjacent to her). She also can use this reaction to deflect a ranged weapon attack against any creature within 15 feet of her; if she succeeds on a DC 14 Charisma saving throw, the winds deflect that attack harmlessly.

HIPPOCAMPUS

This creature has the foreparts of a horse and the hindquarters of a fish. Its forelegs end in splayed fins rather than hooves. A hippocampus's scales vary in color from ivory to deep green to cerulean blue with shades of silver. Aquatic races such as merfolk and locathahs often train hippocampi as steeds or as draft animals used to pull cunningly designed underwater carriages. In the wild, hippocampi prefer to dwell in relatively shallow waters where their favorite food (seaweed and kelp) is more plentiful and larger predators are less common. These creatures often travel in large schools, analogous to free-roaming herds of wild horses on the surface world.

Trainable. The hippocampus is relatively easily trained—the amount of work and cost it requires is equivalent to what it takes to train a horse. Mounted combat on a hippocampus is similar to fighting while riding a horse, although the hippocampus is a clumsy creature on land and cannot move at all out of the water if it has a rider weighing it down.

HIPPOCAMPUS

Large beast, unaligned

Armor Class 11 (natural armor)

Hit Points 15 (2d10+4)

Speed 5 ft., swim 60 ft.

STR	DEX	CON	INT	WIS	CHA
18 (+4)	9 (-1)	14 (+2)	2 (-4)	12 (+1)	11 (+0)

Skills Perception +3

Senses darkvision 60 ft.; passive Perception 13

Languages -

Challenge 1/4 (50 XP)

Hold Breath. A hippocampus can hold its breath up to 15 minutes before it begins suffocation.

Water Breathing. The hippocampus can breathe only underwater.

ACTIONS

Bite. Melee Weapon Attack: +6 to hit, reach 5 ft., one target. *Hit:* 6 (1d4 + 4) piercing damage.

Tail Slap. Melee Weapon Attack: +6 to hit, reach 5 ft., one target. *Hit:* 6 (1d4 + 4) bludgeoning damage.

INCUTILIS

Scholars know life began in the sea, and some— either paranoid or visionary—claim that the sea has manipulated the course of humanoid life through ages beyond reckoning, citing the incutilis as evidence of this. A strange sort of sea creature that appears to be little more than an over-sized cephalopod, an incutilis hides a significant intelligence behind its unassuming appearance. Though most incutilises live their entire lives amid the deepest trenches of the darkest seas, some venture to the border between water and land, revealing terrible control over land-dwelling flesh and an alien disregard for sentient life. Limited in their ability to cross this border and travel on land by their aquatic physiologies, these aberrations overcome this hurdle with a lethal solution, slaying land dwellers and commandeering their flesh to bear the incutilis on shore. To what ends these beings seek to explore the surface remains a mystery—perhaps they do so out of hunger, perhaps out of curiosity, or perhaps because they were sent. A typical incutilis weighs approximately 25 pounds, 30 with its shell, and measures 4 feet from the tips of its longest tentacles to the top of its shell.

Intrusive Controllers. Although incutilises can live as bottom feeders, their favorite foods seem to be higher life forms— sharks, whales, and sentient ocean dwellers—and they appear to make little distinction between the living and the dead, sentient or non-sentient, though usually they avoid dangerous predators and large groups of other sentient beings and preferring instead to operate from the shadows.

Incutilises' most remarkable physical process is their ability to invasively take over dead flesh. So long as a body is relatively intact, the aberration can extend the smaller, more delicate tendrils it typically keeps retracted into its shell. These tendrils are covered with myriad tiny barbs and smaller fibrous filaments it can wind into even the finest internal apertures of a living body with shocking speed and ease. Once the tendrils are in place, the strange chemical laboratory that makes up an incutilis's internal organs allows it to secrete strange chemicals and toxins directly into the body's muscles, causing deliberate contractions, releases, and convulsions that give freshly dead bodies the semblance of life, while those longer dead appear undead. This process requires the incutilis to be latched onto its victim, directing its every motion. If it retracts its tendrils, its host body collapses back into a pile of dead flesh.

INCUTILIS

Tiny aberration, lawful evil

Armor Class 13 (natural armor)

Hit Points 110 (17d4+68)

Speed 5 ft., climb 5 ft., swim 60 ft.

STR	DEX	CON	INT	WIS	CHA
15 (+2)	15 (+2)	18 (+4)	12 (+1)	13 (+1)	8 (−1)

Saving Throws Dex +4

Skills Perception +3, Stealth +6

Senses darkvision 60 ft., passive Perception 13

Languages Aklo, Aquan

Challenge 3 (700 XP)

Amphibious. The incutilis can breathe air and water.

ACTIONS

Tentacle. Melee Weapon Attack. +4 to hit, 5 ft. reach, one target. *Hit:* 24 (4d10 + 2) bludgeoning damage. If the target was a creature, it must make a DC 13 Constitution saving throw or be paralyzed for 1 round.

Ghoulmaster. As an action that provokes opportunity attacks, the incutilis can drive its lesser tendrils into any helpless Small or Medium creature adjacent to it and pump the victim full of poison and chemicals. If the incutilis takes any damage during this process, it is interrupted and stunned until the start of its next turn. The victim must make a DC 13 Constitution saving throw or is killed instantly and becomes a ghoul-like creature under the incutilis's control, using the stats for a ghoul. This ghoul isn't treated as being undead and is immune to spells and effects that affect only undead. The incutilis is attached to this ghoul—typically by the head—occupying the same square and moving along with it. The incutilis can make attacks with its tentacles independently of the ghoul's own attacks. It can also retract its tendrils as a bonus action but doing so causes the ghoul to collapse and revert to a normal corpse. The incutilis must retract its tendrils before it can move away from a ghoul it's attached to. Any attack that deals damage to the ghoul also deals 1 point of damage to the incutilis, regardless of how much damage is dealt to the ghoul. A character can attempt to attack just the incutilis in this state but has disadvantage on the attack roll. Killing the incutilis destroys the ghoul.

INVERTEBRATES

Colorful tentacles writhe across this marine creature like long petals on an immense flower.

Vermin of the Deep. The largest anemones in the ocean are capable predators despite their plodding movement. They lie in fields of other, usually smaller, anemones and among brightly colored coral societies. Deep tiger anemones feed local scavengers by attacking large prey or schools of fish, scattering uneaten remains to their neighbors.

Deep Tiger Anemone

Gargantuan beast, unaligned

Armor Class 15 (natural armor)

Hit Points 248 (15d20 + 90)

Speed 5 ft.

STR	DEX	CON	INT	WIS	CHA
27 (+8)	9 (-1)	22 (+6)	2 (-4)	11 (+0)	10 (+0)

Skills Perception +5, Stealth +4 (+9 in reefs)

Damage Resistances acid

Damage Immunities poison

Condition Immunities blinded, charmed, petrified, poisoned, prone

Senses blindsight 60 ft., passive Perception 15

Languages –

Challenge 14 (11,500 XP)

Acid Cloud. Varinian anemones use concentrated acid to incapacitate and digest their prey. Whenever an anemone suffers a critical hit, or when a creature cuts its way out of the anemone's stomach, the space within the 25-feet is polluted with acid. Creatures who end their turn within this range must succeed on a DC 18 Constitution save or take 3 (1d6) points of acid damage.

Water Breathing. The deep tiger anemone can breathe only underwater.

Actions

Multiattack. The anemone makes three tentacle attacks.

Tentacles. *Melee Weapon Attack:* +13 to hit, reach 15 ft., one target. *Hit:* 34 (4d12 + 8) piercing damage, and the target must make a DC 15 Constitution saving throw, taking 24 (7d6) poison damage and gained the poisoned condition on a failed save, or half as much damage on a successful one. If the target is a Large or smaller creature, it is grappled (escape DC 18). Until this grapple ends, the target is restrained.

Acidic Shards (Recharges 3-6). A deep tiger anemone can fire a barb of crystallized bile at a single target within 60 feet. This crystal begins to dissolve immediately upon exposure to water. The shard deals piercing damage and coats the target's wound with potent acid. The target takes 21 (6d6) points of acid on a failed DC 18 Dexterity saving throw or half as much on a success. The damage continues on the following round regardless if the save was successful or not, with the target taking a further 10 (3d6) points of acid damage, and 3 (1d6) more the round after that.

Reaction

Digest. If at the end of its turn the anemone has a creature grappled it may swallow the creature whole if it is Large or smaller. It may swallow any number of grappled creatures with this reaction. A swallowed creature is blinded and restrained, it has total cover against attacks and other effects outside the anemone, and it takes 28 (8d6) bludgeoning damage at the start of each of the anemone's turns. If the anemone takes 29 damage or more on a single turn from a creature inside it, the anemone must succeed on a DC 20 Constitution saving throw at the end of that turn or regurgitate all swallowed creatures, which fall prone in a space within 10 feet of the anemone. This also triggers its acid cloud ability. If the anemone dies, a swallowed creature is no longer restrained by it and can escape from the corpse by using 20 feet of movement, exiting prone.

DIRE SEASTAR

Muscular tentacles explode from the sand and fold inward toward a toothless central maw.

Creeping Doom. Some starfish contend with a greater number of more dangerous marine threats than their lesser king, driving evolution to produce faster and stronger specimens (or the survival of deadly primordial species) that attack aggressively and recover from injury very quickly. Most unique among the seastars of the deep ocean and deadly coasts are those with no agenda or reproductive mechanism other than to split and regenerate after attacked by predators. Ironically, the number of natural enemies that find them delicious ensures their survival.

One too Many Mouths. Varinaian seastars have mouths on both sides of their bodies, allowing them to crawl towards stationary food, or to lies half-buried in sand to ambush prey crawling across the seabed above them. The average dire seastar is 7 feet in diameter and weighs 600 pounds.

DIRE SEASTAR

Large beast, unaligned

Armor Class 15 (natural armor)

Hit Points 104 (11d10 + 44)

Speed 10 ft., climb 10 ft.

STR	DEX	CON	INT	WIS	CHA
17 (+3)	15 (+2)	18 (+4)	8 (-1)	13 (+1)	8 (-1)

Saving Throws Dex +5, Wis +4, Cha +2

Condition Immunities prone

Damage Resistance bludgeoning

Senses blindsight 30 ft., passive Perception 11

Languages -

Challenge 6 (2,300 XP)

Regeneration. The seastar regains 5 hit points at the start of its turn. If the seastar takes acid or fire damage, this trait doesn't function at the start of the seastar's next turn. The seastar dies only if it starts its turn with 0 hit points and doesn't regenerate.

Tube Feet. Dire seastars move and grapple using thousands of shorter appendages filled with fluid and ending in tiny suction cups. They treat any solid surface as clear terrain. They also have advantage on Strength (Athletics) checks against being shoved, and on saving throws against any effect that would force it to move.

Water Breathing. The seastar can breathe only underwater.

ACTIONS

Multiattack. The seastar makes two slam attacks.

Slam. *Melee Weapon Attack:* +6 to hit, reach 15 ft., one target. *Hit:* 14 (2d10 + 3) bludgeoning damage, and if the target is a Medium or smaller creature and the seastar isn't already grappling a creature, it is grappled (escape DC 12).

External Stomach. A dire seastar ejects its stomach in order to begin digestion of a captured meal. If the target is a Medium or smaller creature grappled by the seastar, that creature is digested, and the grapple ends. While being digested, the creature is blinded and restrained, it has total cover against attacks and other effects outside the seastar's external stomach, and it takes 14 (4d6) acid damage at the start of each of the seastar's turns. If the seastar's external stomach takes 20 damage or more on a single turn from a creature inside it, the seastar must succeed on a DC 14 Constitution saving throw at the end of that turn or regurgitate all swallowed creatures, which fall prone in a space within 5 feet of the seastar. Damage done to a seastar's stomach does not harm the seastar. If the seastar dies, a swallowed creature is no longer restrained by it and can escape from the corpse using 5 feet of movement, exiting prone.

REACTION

Split. When a dire seastar is subjected to a critical hit from a slashing attack, it splits into two new seastars if it has at least 10 hit points. Each new seastar has hit points equal to half the original seastar's, rounded down. New seastar are one size smaller than the original seastar.

GIANT URCHINS

Much more dangerous than their smaller kin, giant sea urchins are dangerous predators of opportunity.

Amphibious Hunters. Hunter urchins can adjust their spines to effect an awkward method of locomotion on land. They use their tethered hook-spines to draw their prey close enough to stab it into submission and then devour it.

Ravenous Urchins. Unlike most urchins, the creatures that make up the infamous urchin swarms are capable of propelling themselves beneath the waves at furious speeds, creating a dangerous threat to pearl divers and other aquatic creatures, piercing them not only with their venomous spines but also with their rasping tongues. This menace of the reefs and tide pools is often dismissed as a myth until it's far too late.

Hunter Urchin

Medium beast, unaligned

Armor Class 13 (natural armor)

Hit Points 52 (8d8+16)

Speed 5 ft., swim 15 ft.

STR	DEX	CON	INT	WIS	CHA
15 (+2)	3 (-4)	14 (+2)	1 (-5)	12 (+1)	2 (-4)

Skills Perception +3

Senses passive Perception 13

Challenge 1/2 (100 XP)

Amphibious. Hunter urchins can breathe both air and water.

Stability. Hunter urchins can anchor themselves to rocky surfaces on any turn in which they do not move. Until they release their hold, they have advantage on Strength (Athletics) checks against being shoved, and on saving throws against any effect that would force it to move. As long as it does not move on its turn, its Dexterity penalty does not apply as a penalty on its attack roll with its tethered spine.

Actions

Tethered Spine. Ranged Weapon Attack: +4 to hit, range 15 ft., one target. *Hit:* 4 (1d4 + 2) piercing damage and the target is pulled 5 feet closer to the urchin.

Spines. Melee Weapon Attack: +4 to hit, range 5 ft., one target. *Hit:* 2 (1d4) piercing damage and the target must make a DC 13 Constitution saving throw or be poisoned for 1 minute.

Reaction

Spiny Defense. When a creature makes a melee attack against the hunter urchin, as a reaction it can make a spines attack against that creature. It can use this reaction up to 3 times per round.

Ravenous Urchin Swarm

Medium swarm of Tiny beasts, unaligned

Armor Class 13 (natural armor)

Hit Points 72 (16d8)

Speed 0 ft., swim 20 ft.

STR	DEX	CON	INT	WIS	CHA
1 (-5)	12 (+1)	10 (+0)	4 (-3)	13 (+1)	9 (-1)

Senses passive Perception 11

Languages -

Challenge 1 (200 XP)

Jet. While underwater, a ravenous urchin swarm can Dash as a bonus action and does not provoke opportunity attacks while jetting. It must move in a straight line when it uses this action.

Spiky. Each time a creature attacks the urchin swarm in melee with an unarmed attack or a natural weapon like a claw or bite, or attempts to grapple or Shove the swarm, takes 1 piercing damage and 2 (1d4) poison damage.

Swarm. The swarm can occupy someone else's space and vice versa. The swarm can fit into any space large enough for a tiny urchin to squeeze through and can use a reaction to attack any creature that leaves its square with an attack of opportunity.

Underfoot. Any area containing the swarm is treated as difficult terrain, and creatures swimming or walking through the swarm must make a DC 11 Dexterity saving throw or affected by its Spiky ability.

Water Breathing. Ravenous urchins can breathe only underwater; however, they can hold seawater inside their bodies when the tide goes out, allowing them to survive until it returns.

Actions

Spiny Swarm. Melee Weapon Attack: +3 to hit, range 5 feet, one target. *Hit:* 3 (1d4+1) piercing damage and 7 (2d6) poison damage, or half as much on a successful DC 13 Constitution saving throw. Creatures failing their saving throw also become poisoned. They can end the poisoned effect with a DC 13 Constitution save each round at the end of their turn, but while poisoned have their speed is reduced by half.

JELLYFISH

Unlike their smaller cousins, giant jellyfish are active predators that seek out prey. Capable of slithering through narrow cracks, a giant jellyfish is a horrifying beast to encounter lurking in the hold of a flooded or sunken ship. Other species of these vermin exist, as summarized on the following table—these variants often have different types of poison or other abilities like translucency or constriction.

Blood Feeders. The crimson jellyfish is a blood-drinking creature whose red color comes from the blood absorbed throughout its body after it feeds. A large fish or sea mammal encountering a pack or bloom of these creatures can be drained of blood in a matter of minutes. Fortunately, a crimson jellyfish's bright color makes it fairly easy to avoid under well-lit conditions.

Deadly Drifters. Jellyfish often cluster together during springtime or when environmental conditions such as an increase in ocean temperature favor it. When conditions are right, jellyfish shift from being a nuisance to being a menace, if accidentally so, for a jellyfish swarm, unlike more aggressive monstrous kin like the giant jellyfish, comprises not aggressive hunters but rather opportunistic strikers. They do not generally move to attack nearby prey, but their nearly translucent coloration makes it horrifically easy for a creature to swim into a swarm unawares. Once a jellyfish swarm deals damage to a creature, the swarm pursues it for several rounds before giving up the chase. Many aquatic races use jellyfish swarms as defensive guardians, trusting a swarm's lack of interest in moving to keep it stationary for long periods of time.

Sapphire Stalkers. Sapphire jellyfish are active hunters. They store powerful electrical charges in their domelike bells, which are 16 feet in diameter. Their sensory tentacles can trail for twice that length, but the dangerous toxic tentacles are positioned within about 20 feet of the creature's bell.

CRIMSON JELLYFISH

Medium beast, unaligned

Armor Class 14 (natural armor)

Hit Points 120 (16d8+48)

Speed swim 10 ft.

STR	DEX	CON	INT	WIS	CHA
4 (−3)	13 (+1)	16 (+3)	2 (−4)	13 (+1)	1 (−5)

Saving Throws Con +5

Skills Stealth +3

Damage Resistances bludgeoning

Damage Immunities poison

Condition Immunities charmed, frightened, poisoned

Senses darkvision 60 ft., passive Perception 11

Languages –

Challenge 4 (1,100 XP)

Water Breathing. The crimson jellyfish can only breathe underwater.

ACTIONS

Multiattack. The crimson jellyfish makes two tentacle attacks.

Tentacle. *Melee Weapon Attack.* +3 to hit, 10 ft. reach, one target. *Hit:* 13 (3d8) poison damage. If the target was a creature it must succeed a DC 14 Constitution saving throw or be poisoned for 1 minute.

Jellyfish, Sapphire

Huge beast, unaligned

Armor Class 17 (natural armor)

Hit Points 121 (9d12+63)

Speed swim 30 ft.

STR	DEX	CON	INT	WIS	CHA
6 (–2)	19 (+4)	24 (+7)	2 (–4)	13 (+1)	1 (–5)

Saving Throws Con +11, Dex +8

Skills Stealth +8

Damage Resistances bludgeoning

Damage Immunities poison, lightning

Condition Immunities charmed, frightened, poisoned

Senses darkvision 60 ft., passive Perception 11

Languages –

Challenge 11 (7,200 XP)

Water Breathing. The sapphire jellyfish can only breathe underwater.

Actions

Multiattack. The sapphire jellyfish makes four tentacle attacks.

Tentacle. *Melee Weapon Attack.* +8 to hit, 20 ft. reach, one target. *Hit:* 18 (4d8) poison damage. If the target was a creature it must succeed a DC 17 Constitution saving throw or be poisoned for 1 minute.

Electricity Blast (Recharges 5–6). The sapphire jellyfish can unleash a blast of electricity within a radius of 20 feet. Each creature within this radius must succeed a DC 17 Dexterity saving throw or take 18 (4d8) lightning damage and be stunned for 1 round.

Jellyfish Swarm

Large swarm of Tiny beasts, unaligned

Armor Class 15 (natural armor)

Hit Points 120 (16d8+48)

Speed swim 20 ft.

STR	DEX	CON	INT	WIS	CHA
1 (–15)	13 (+1)	14 (+2)	2 (–4)	13 (+1)	1 (–5)

Saving Throws Con +5

Skills Stealth +4

Damage Resistances bludgeoning

Damage Immunities poison

Condition Immunities charmed, frightened, grappled, paralyzed, petrified, prone, restrained, stunned

Senses darkvision 60 ft., passive Perception 11

Languages –

Challenge 6 (2,300 XP)

Swarm. The swarm can occupy another creature's space and vice versa, and the swarm can move through any opening large enough for a Tiny jellyfish. The swarm can't regain hit points or gain temporary hit points..

Water Breathing. The jellyfish swarm can only breathe underwater.

Actions

Mass of Tentacles. *Melee Weapon Attack.* +4 to hit, 0 ft. reach, two targets in the swarm's space. *Hit:* 21 (6d6) poison damage. If the target was a creature it must succeed a DC 15 Constitution saving throw or be poisoned for 1 minute.

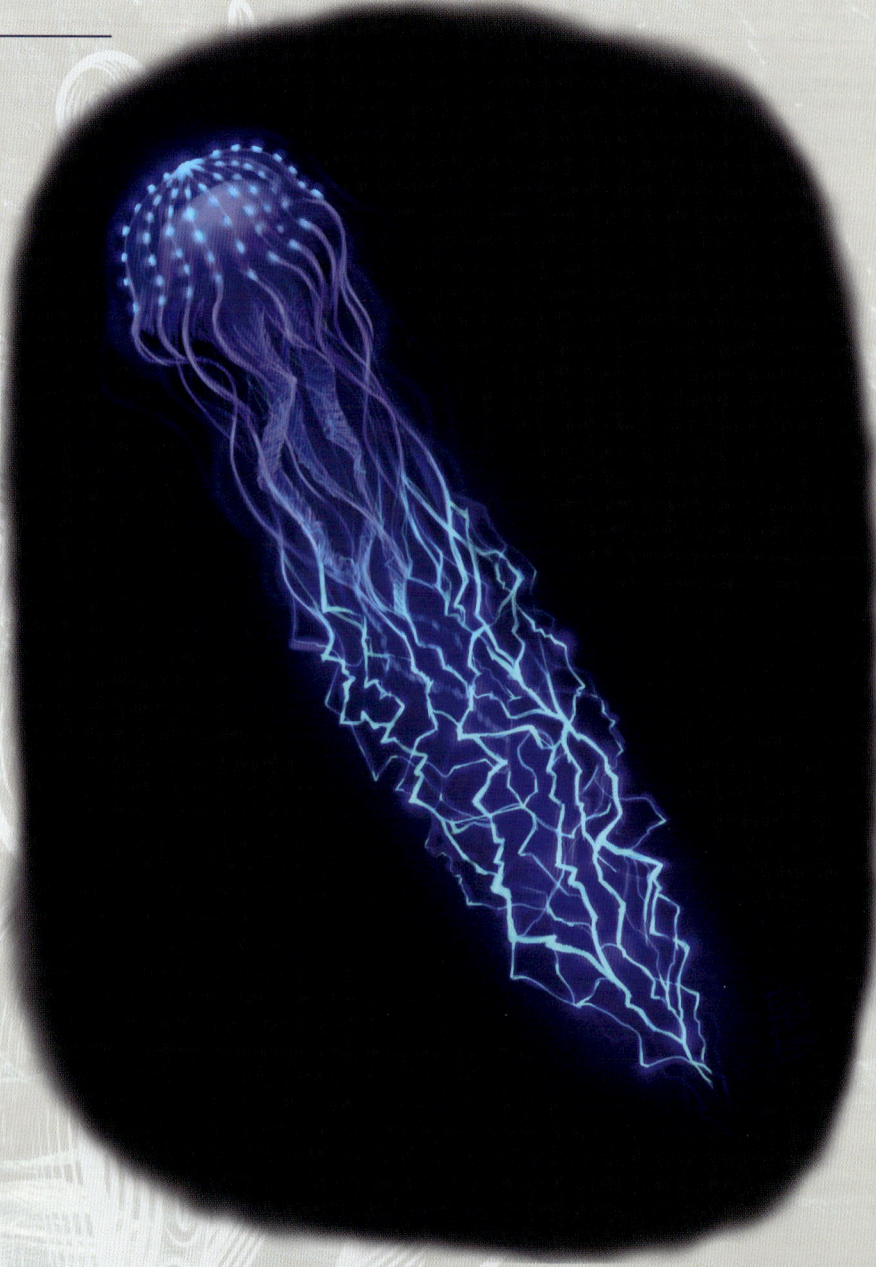

JORGANTH

Jorganths are otherworldly eel-serpents, invaders from beyond into the deepest and darkest reaches of the oceans on the homeworld of the player characters. At first glance they appear basically reptilian, though they combine wormlike and piscine features with insectile appendages and sensory organs. They are fierce predators and cunning hunters, able to track down their prey wherever they hide. An adult jorganth is nearly 20 feet long and weighs 1 ton.

Fey or Fiend. The jorganth is an otherworldly abomination of uncertain origins. They are found in numbers in the benighted ocean depths of the fey realms, where the joyous revels of aquatic faeries were never seen. There they feed upon the weaker inhabitants of the boundless reefs and pelagic abysms, as common camouflage and the glamours of the fey and their fey-touched pets are of no use against its hyperacute senses. However, they may not be native to the realms of Faerie, arriving instead by a chance transpatial thinness or rupture from a far-distant planet or dimension. Their advent occurred so far below the faerie seas that it went unnoticed for many long years, time enough for the jorganths to grow and multiply, such that even the mightiest hunters of the fey lords could never eradicate the nests of these alien predators. The rulers of the fey sought to lure these vicious beasts out of their own waters by enticing them into richer hunting grounds in the material world through planar vortices of their own, but while some took the bait enough remained that the threat was truly ended in neither place but instead now spread into the deep trenches of the mortal seafloor, there to once more seed new oceans with their terrifying progeny.

Feed on Fear. Jorganth are psychic parasites, scavenging the naked terror of the creatures it hunts with an avid glee and tormenting it with hit-and-run attacks, disappearing in the gloom and lurking just out of sight, only to rush in again bringing agony and panic in its wake. Their alien psychophysiology appears to require the consumption of this psychic fodder as well as physical provender in order for them to grow, and jorganths are certainly not above preying on their own kind. In fact, jorganths learn well the meaning of fear trying to survive their larval stages, as most are devoured by their kin before reaching adulthood. This cannibalistic terrorism is perhaps why the species has never risen beyond the level of lurking terror in the depths to become a true threat to the civilized races above.

Saltmarsh Jorganth. It is rare but not unheard of for jorganth to abandon the deep waters and crawl up onto the continental shelf and coastal reef waters, and thence even into tidewaters, bays, saltwater sloughs, and similar coastal wetlands. These jorganth are much like their deep-dwelling kin, but they are able to give birth to standard flying will-o'-wisps rather than will-o'-the-deeps.

Jorganth

Large aberration, chaotic evil

Armor Class 16 (natural armor)

Hit Points 180 (19d10+76)

Speed 10 ft., swim 60 ft.

STR	DEX	CON	INT	WIS	CHA
22 (+6)	15 (+2)	19 (+4)	11 (+0)	14 (+2)	13 (+1)

Saving Throws Str +9, Con +7

Skills Athletics +9, Perception +8

Damage Resistance cold

Damage Immunities lightning

Senses darkvision 60 ft., tremorsense 60 ft., passive Perception 18

Languages Aklo, Aquan

Challenge 8 (3,900 XP)

Electric Field. A jorganth has a passive electric field surrounding it with a radius of 30 feet. Any creatures wearing metal armor or using a metal weapon takes 7 (2d6) lightning damage at the start of their turns while in this electric field.

Innate Spellcasting. A jorganth's spellcasting ability is Charisma (spell save DC 12). It can innately cast the following spells, requiring no material components:

At will: *dancing lights*

Water Breathing. A jorganth can only breathe underwater.

Actions

Multiattack. The jorganth makes one bite attack and two tentacle attacks.

Bite. Melee Weapon Attack. +9 to hit, 10 ft. reach, one target. *Hit:* 13 (2d6 + 6) piercing damage.

Tentacle. Melee Weapon Attack. +9 to hit, 10 ft. reach, one target. *Hit:* 9 (1d6 + 6) bludgeoning damage plus 14 (4d6) lightning damage.

Hyper Beam. The jorganth can fire off an explosive beam of lightning 5 feet wide and 120 feet long. Any creatures caught in this beam must succeed a DC 16 Dexterity saving throw or take 13 (3d8) lightning damage. When a jorganth uses this ability, its Electric Field trait shuts off for 1 round.

Will-o'-the-Deep. The jorganth can shut off its Electric Field trait in order to summon a will-o'-wisp within 30 feet of itself. This will-o'-wisp has a swim speed of 50 feet and is completely loyal to the jorganth. Once this will-o'-wisp is summoned, the jorganth must wait 1 minute before its Electric Field trait turns back on.

KARKINOI

Monstrous hunters and bullies of the ocean depths, karkinoi are hulking crab-like humanoid brutes that live only to destroy creatures that dare cross their path and then feed on the corpses of the vanquished. While karkinoi can walk on land, they do not enjoy long periods away from the sea, as they dry out, crack, and eventually suffocate. Karkinoi stand over 9 feet tall and weigh over 800 pounds.

Brutal. Though not mindless, they have no inclination to build civilizations or even settlements, living in roving gangs or nomadic tribes. The tools they use in their more humanoid appendages are always scavenged, usually from victims, and are discarded when broken or of no more immediate use. Pursuits such as crafting, learning, and diplomacy are a waste to them; they see these as the activities of food-creatures not strong enough to see the world as it is—a stage for domination, feeding, and spawning. Even when these brutes band together, it is usually to spawn or to face sources of food that are too strong for only one or two karkinoi alone.

Shore Raiders. Large hordes of karkinoi come together to hunt inhabitants of coastal settlements. Striking at night, they do as much damage as possible before dragging their meals into the sea. They make such attacks night after night until the settlement is destroyed or the resistance becomes too fierce, at which point the horde disbands and each karkinoi makes its own way in the sea.

Coastal raids are part of the karkinoi breeding cycle. The corpses that they drag off into the ocean are tethered to masses of eggs and serve as food for karkinoi spawn. The spawn develop a taste for land-meat and crave it, ensuring the next generation of hungry raiders.

Karkinoi

Large humanoid (karkinoi), chaotic evil

Armor Class 15 (natural armor)

Hit Points 153 (18d10+54)

Speed 30 ft., swim 40 ft.

STR	DEX	CON	INT	WIS	CHA
22 (+6)	10 (+0)	16 (+3)	6 (–2)	10 (+0)	7 (–2)

Saving Throws Con +6, Str +9

Skills Athletics +9, Perception +6

Senses darkvision 60 ft., passive Perception 16

Languages Aquan

Challenge 6 (2,300 XP)

Constrict. A karkinoi can only have two creatures grappled at once. If a creature is grappled by the karkinoi at the beginning of its turn, it takes 22 (4d6+6) bludgeoning damage.

Sideways Scuttle. Whenever the karkinoi takes the Dash action, it can move twice its normal movement speed.

Water Dependency. A karkinoi can only breathe underwater but can hold its breath out of water for 3 hours.

Actions

Multiattack. The karkinoi makes two claw attacks.

Claw. *Melee Weapon Attack.* +9 to hit, 10 ft. reach, one target. *Hit:* 19 (3d8 + 6) bludgeoning damage. Instead of dealing damage, the karkinoi can grapple the target (escape DC 15).

LASHER SCALLOP

Found in sea caves, shaded hollows along tidal shelves, and mangrove swamps, lasher scallops are agile and curious cephalopods that are equally at home on land and in the water. Their five tentacles are ideal for climbing around the tangled environs of the tunnels and forested hummocks, while their sharp eyes are able to penetrate the gloom of thick-canopied swamps and caverns alike. With strong limbs and an incredibly sharp beak they hunt insects, small mammals, as well as fallen fruit and mushrooms. Quick and ever alert for danger, lasher scallops flee larger predators when they must, but if threatened without the opportunity to escape they grab onto any available surface and retreat completely into their shell, offering no soft point for a potential threat to attack.

A lasher scallop measures three feet across without counting its tentacles and weighs 150 lbs.

Intelligent Bivalves. Extremely intelligent animals, lasher scallops commonly fashion simple tools from rocks and sticks and have been observed to have complex problem-solving skills. Social beasts, they can often be found in small family groups, or routs, that travel and forage together. Naturally capable of metachrosis—the ability to change their pigmentation—they express their emotions via complex color bursts and patterns on their skin and can make whistling calls channeled through their shells to communicate over long distances.

Egg Layers. Lasher scallops reproduce by laying eggs, which the female will typically attach to the bottoms of roots, cave shelves, or tree limbs where the rout is nesting. The eggs take eight to twelve months to hatch, and stars can spawn roughly once a year, with the entire rout guarding the clutch. Lasher scallops mature within 5-7 years but rarely live beyond 20.

Curious Collectors. More curious than cautious, lasher scallops quickly overcome any fear they might have of the trappings of civilization. Attracted to the sounds and smells, they can be found around settlements of any size, and are particularly drawn to dumps and trash heaps for the easy foraging. Natural problem solvers with clever appendages, they are regarded as something of a nuisance as few places can be considered truly 'lasher scallop proof' from the always hungry little omnivores. Nothing short of a locked metal box can keep a lasher scallop away from provisions once it has caught the scent of them, and some naturalists joke that it is only a matter of time before the cephalopods figure out how to pick locks. It is not unusual for lasher scallops to steal other items as well, as they have an insatiable fascination with bright shiny things, which they invariably bring back to the rout nest.

LASHER SCALLOP

Small beast, unaligned

Armor Class 13

Hit Points 44 (8d6+16)

Speed 30 ft., climb 30 ft.

STR	DEX	CON	INT	WIS	CHA
14 (+2)	17 (+3)	14 (+2)	2 (-4)	14 (+2)	3 (-4)

Senses darkvision 60 ft., passive Perception 12

Languages -

Challenge 1/2 (100 XP)

ACTIONS

Multiattack. The lasher scallop makes three tentacle attacks.

Tentacle. *Melee Weapon Attack:* +4 to hit, reach 5 ft., one target. *Hit:* 3 (1d3 + 2) bludgeoning damage and the target must make a DC 13 Dexterity saving throw or the lasher's tentacle sticks to it (escape DC 13). While stuck, the lasher scallop has advantage on attack rolls against the target and the target has disadvantage on Dexterity saving throws. The scallop can still use these stuck tentacles to attack, but only against the stuck target by constricting it. If all three of its tentacles are stuck, it no longer can make attacks of opportunity.

Shell Retreat. The lasher scallop can retreat into its shell, making it much harder to strike. While in its shell the lasher scallop is AC 18 but its speed is 0.

Reappear. The lasher scallop can come out from its shell, regaining its normal armor class and the ability to move.

LASIODON

Lasiodons are something out of ancient nightmares, with whale-like bodies, powerful fluked tails, and thick fins surmounted by six long-necked heads. Above each head's nightmarish maw is a curved, fleshy growth that glows in the dark waters with a pale radiance.

Deep Hydras. Lasiodons hunt the deepest oceans, luring inquisitive prey with the white glow of their protruding anglers and devouring it whole. With teeth able to slice solid stone, a lasiodon can freeze its quarry, sometimes attacking a school of large fish by freezing some and devouring others. In the darkest coldest depths, blocks of ice created by the creature's breath weapon remain still for several seconds before ascending slowly. Adult lasiodons average 60 feet long and weigh over 50 tons.

Unlimited Growth. Lasiodons never stop growing and seem immune to the effects of aging. Adult females average 60 feet long and weigh over 50 tons.

Lone Hunter. Lasiodons are cunning but not intelligent or social. The ferocious predators require a large hunting area, so they are almost always alone when encountered. They mate every few years at particularly bountiful hunting grounds in a frenzy that turns the ocean's green waters red.

LASIODON

Gargantuan monstrosity, unaligned

Armor Class 19 (natural armor)

Hit Points 330 (21d20+105)

Speed 0 ft., swim 50 ft.

STR	DEX	CON	INT	WIS	CHA
26 (+8)	10 (+0)	18 (+5)	2 (-4)	10 (+0)	7 (-2)

Saving Throws Dex +6, Con +11

Skills Perception +6, Stealth +6 (+12 if submerged)

Damage Resistances bludgeoning, piercing, and slashing from nonmagical attacks

Damage Immunities cold

Senses darkvision 120 ft., passive Perception 16

Languages —

Challenge 18 (20,000 XP)

Multiple Heads. The lasiodon has six heads. While it has more than one head, the lasiodon has advantage on saving throws against being blinded, charmed, deafened, frightened, stunned, and knocked unconscious. Whenever the lasiodon takes 55 or more damage in a single turn, one of its heads dies.

Reactive Heads. For each head, the lasiodon has beyond one, it gets an extra reaction that can be used only for opportunity attacks.

Keen Smell. The lasiodon has advantage on Wisdom (Perception) checks that rely on smell.

Black See. A lasiodon sees perfectly in darkness, including magical darkness. Each of its six heads protrudes a fleshy appendage that can project natural luminescence or shadow. Once each round as a bonus action, the lasiodon determines how many heads to light up to illuminate an area, increasing the illumination in a 10-foot sphere per head. If none of its heads project light, it can instead project magical *darkness* (as the spell). Each head then reduces the illumination level to total darkness in a 60-foot sphere.

Camouflage. A lasiodon can spread itself out over a large area with its long necks and immense torso. It changes color to match the waters it swims in and moves with aquatic grace. While submerged, a lasiodon has advantage on Dexterity (Stealth) checks.

Water Breathing. The lasiodon can breathe only underwater.

ACTIONS

Multiattack. The lasiodon makes as many bite attacks as it has heads. At full health, a lasiodon has six.

Bite. *Melee Weapon Attack.* +14 to hit, reach 25 ft., one target. Hit: 24 (3d10 + 8) piercing damage. If the target is a Large or smaller creature, it must succeed on a DC 19 Dexterity saving throw or be swallowed by the lasiodon. A swallowed creature is blinded and restrained, it has total cover against attacks and other effects outside the lasiodon, and it takes 21 (6d6) acid damage at the start of each of the lasiodon's turns. If the lasiodon takes 33 damage or more on a single turn from a creature inside it, the lasiodon must succeed on a DC 22 Constitution saving throw at the end of that turn or regurgitate all swallowed creatures, which fall prone in a space within 10 feet of the lasiodon. If the lasiodon dies, a swallowed creature is no longer restrained by it and can escape from the corpse by using 20 feet of movement, exiting prone.

Frigid Breath (Recharge 5–6). The lasiodon exhales an icy blast in a 90-foot cone. Each creature in that area must make a DC 19 Constitution saving throw, taking 67 (15d8) cold damage on a failed save, or half as much damage on a successful one. Creatures that fail the saving throw are also encased in ice and gain the restrained condition until the ice melts or is destroyed. The ice has Armor Class 15 and 33 Hit Points, and damage from all effects other than magical fire and adamantine weapons is reduced by 5 points per attack. If the ice is created under water the target floats upward 60 feet each round at the beginning of its turn.

REACTION

Frozen Food. When the lasiodon is reduced to less than half its original hit points its frigid breath attack option recharges and it may use it as a reaction.

LEGENDARY ACTIONS

A lasiodon can take 3 legendary actions, choosing from the options below. Only one legendary action option can be used at a time and only at the end of another creature's turn. A lasiodon regains spent legendary actions at the start of its turn.

Move. The lasiodon moves up to half its speed.

Shroud. The lasiodon radiates magical *darkness* (as the spell) in a 30-foot radius. The darkness lasts until the start of the lasiodon's next turn.

Bite (Costs 2 Actions). The lasiodon makes one bite attack.

LESHY, SEAWEED

Seaweed leshies usually dwell along coastlines, happily splashing and playing in tide pools, but they are equally at home at sea, floating among large kelp beds. Although perfectly capable of existing out of water indefinitely, seaweed leshies prefer to limit their time away from the sea almost out of a sense of pride. Most seaweed leshies take a dim view of freshwater plant life, to the point of mocking such plants in the same way an urbanite might talk down to folk who live in more rural areas. Rumors of freshwater leshies are a sure way to bring peals of mocking laughter from a seaweed leshy.

Seaweed leshies resemble miniature, waterlogged green humans grown from leafy green seaweed, with skinny arms and legs, webbed hands and feet, and long strands of brown, green, or red seaweed for hair. They wear armor made from a pair of large clam shells or from several smaller shells tied together. This armor functions for a seaweed leshy, but not for any other creature.

Patient and thoughtful by inclination (save for matters associated with those silly freshwater leshies), seaweed leshies believe that in time nature brings what is needed by the ebb and flow of the tide or the steady flow of the river. They counsel against hasty decisions and rash actions, always preferring to wait and see what another day might bring.

Guardians of Plant Life. Originally grown as servants for more powerful fey and intelligent plant life such as elder treants, leshies are sentient plants who look after their unintelligent brethren and serve as nature's verdant watchers. Several breeds of leshy exist, each being kindred to a broad group of plants or fungi. Leshies begin their existence as sentient though bodiless spirits of nature of the sort contacted by spells such as commune with nature. These spirits normally have no way to directly manipulate the physical world, but a skilled spellcaster (typically a druid) can grow a special plant body for one of these spirits, giving the spirit a home to animate.

Embodied Spirits. Once accepted into a body, a leshy's spirit remains within unless the body is destroyed. Leshies do not fear death as many other creatures do, knowing that should they fall, their spirits merely return to the natural world and can be called to inhabit a new leshy body at some point in the future. As a leshy's body dies, the magic animating it unravels in a burst of life energy that infuses its surrounding and quickens the growth of any plants in the vicinity. Some leshies even voluntarily discorporate to save the lives of ailing plants, knowing that their sacrifice may mean the continuation of countless otherwise helpless flora. Regardless of how a leshy dies, leaving the body traumatizes the spirit, and the leshy retains only faint memories of past corporeal existences. Leshy spirits need not return to the same form if bound again to a body. Throughout its existence, a single spirit can inhabit any number of different types of leshies. A leshy without a body has no power to affect or contact the material world.

Unique. The rites and special materials required to create a leshy's physical form vary between individual leshies. Once the creator assembles the necessary materials, a leshy must typically be grown in an area of natural power, such as a treant's grove, a druidic circle, or a site of pristine natural wonder. A newly born leshy is a free-willed, neutral being, under no obligation to serve its creator.

SEAWEED LESHY

Small plant, neutral

Armor Class 12 (armor)
Hit Points 26 (4d6+12)
Speed 20 ft., swim 20 ft.

STR	DEX	CON	INT	WIS	CHA
10 (+0)	13 (+1)	16 (+3)	9 (-1)	15 (+2)	12 (+1)

Damage Resistances lightning, thunder
Skills Perception +4, Stealth +5, Survival +4

Senses darkvision 60 ft.; passive Perception 14

Languages Druidic, Sylvan

Challenge 1/4 (50 XP)

Air Cyst. Seaweed leshys constantly grow small bulbs filled with air. As an action, they can detach a bulb and give it to another creature. If consumed as an action, this air cyst grants the ability to breathe both air and water for 10 minutes. Seaweed leshys can have a maximum of four usable air cysts at any one time, and air cysts regrow at a rate of one per 24 hours.

Amphibious. A seaweed leshy breathes air and water.

Pass Without Trace. In areas of natural vegetation, a leshy can't be tracked except by magical means. The leshy leaves behind no tracks or other traces of its passage.

Seaweed Speech. Seaweed leshys can communicate with seaweed, asking it about events within the past day, gaining information about creatures that have passed, weather, and other circumstances, within a radius of 30 feet.

Verdant Burst. When slain, a leshy explodes in a burst of fertile energies. All plant creatures within 30 feet of the slain leshy regain 6 (1d8+2) hit points, and seaweed quickly infests the area. If the terrain can support the growth of seaweed, the undergrowth is dense enough to make the region into difficult terrain for 24 hours, after which the plant life diminishes to a normal level; otherwise, the plant life has no significant effect on movement and withers and dies within an hour.

ACTIONS

Slam. *Melee Weapon Attack:* +3 to hit, reach 5 ft., one target. *Hit:* 4 (1d6+1) bludgeoning damage.

Water Jet. *Ranged Weapon Attack:* +3 to hit, range 30/60 ft., one target. *Hit:* 1 bludgeoning damage, and the target must make a DC 15 Constitution saving throw. On a failure, the target is blinded until the beginning of the leshy's next turn.

Change Shape. The seaweed leshy can take the shape of seaweed or return to its normal form. In seaweed form it is not capable of any other actions but is aware of its surroundings. It is otherwise indistinguishable from ordinary seaweed. Any items it carries fall to the ground when it becomes seaweed, but when it returns to its normal form it easily dons its armor at the same time.

Seaweed. Grasping seaweed sprouts from the ground in a 20-foot square starting from a point within 90 feet that is in saltwater. For 1 minute, the seaweed turns the ground and water in the area into difficult terrain. A creature in the area when the leshy uses seaweed must succeed on a DC 12 Strength saving throw or be restrained by the entangling seaweed until the spell ends. A creature restrained by the seaweed can use its action to make a Strength check against the same DC. On a success, it frees itself. After 1 minute, the conjured seaweed wilts away.

LINNORM, FJORD

Fjord linnorms are massive eel-like dragons with two webbed talons and a tail ending in large and powerful flukes. They dwell among the deep waters that grace polar coastlines where fingers of land create complex rivulets, venturing out to sea to feed on sharks and whales when they cannot find settlements or trading ships to savage. As their favored haunts often overlap with coastal trade routes, regions known to be within the territory of a fjord linnorm are often avoided by ships. Fjord linnorms are not particularly adept at capsizing ships, as are some other large aquatic monsters, but one might argue that such tactics are unnecessary for a creature the size and power of a fjord linnorm in the first place.

FJORD LINNORM

Gargantuan dragon (linnorm), chaotic evil

Armor Class 21 (natural armor)

Hit Points 246 (16d20+80)

Speed 30 ft., fly 70 ft., swim 70 ft.

STR	DEX	CON	INT	WIS	CHA
25 (+7)	18 (+4)	21 (+5)	5 (-3)	17 (+3)	20 (+5)

Saving Throws Str +14, Con +12, Int +4, Wis +10, Cha +12

Skills Athletics +14, Perception +10

Damage Resistances bludgeoning, piercing, and slashing from nommagical attacks

Damage Immunities cold

Senses darkvision 60 ft., blindsight 60 ft., truesight 60 ft.; passive Perception 20

Languages Draconic, Sylvan

Challenge 21 (33,000 XP)

Amphibious. The fjord linnorm can breathe air and water.

Death Curse: Drowning. If a creature reduces a fjord linnorm to 0 hit points or kills it outright, the creature must make a DC 20 Wisdom saving throw. On a failed save, the creature suffers from the curse of drowning. The cursed creature loses the ability to breathe water and cannot gain that ability; in addition, a creature that can hold its breath can hold its breath only half as long.

Immunity to Curses. The linnorm automatically succeeds on saving throws against curses.

Legendary Resistance (3/Day). If the linnorm fails a saving throw, it can choose to succeed instead.

ACTIONS

Multiattack. The linnorm makes three attacks: one with its bite and two with its claws. It can use constrict in place of one claw attack.

Bite. *Melee Weapon Attack:* +11 to hit, reach 15 ft., one target. *Hit:* 16 (2d8+7) piercing damage, plus 10 (3d6) cold and 10 (3d6) poison damage.

Claw. *Melee Weapon Attack:* +11 to hit, reach 10 ft., one target. *Hit:* 13 (2d6+7) slashing damage.

Constrict. *Melee Weapon Attack:* +11 to hit, reach 20 ft., one target. *Hit:* 13 (2d6+7) bludgeoning damage and the target is grappled (escape DC 24). Until this grapple ends, the creature is restrained, and the linnorm can't use constrict on another target.

Icy Breath (Recharge 5–6): The linnorm expels poisonous icy fluid in a 120-foot line that is a 5-feet wide. Each creature in that area must make a DC 20 Constitution saving throw, taking 72 (16d8) poison damage on a failed save, or half as much damage on a successful one. On a failed saving throw, the freezing liquid quickly hardens to sheets of ice, causing the creature to be restrained for 1 minute. On its turn, a restrained creature can use its action to make a DC 20 Strength check, freeing itself on a success.

LEGENDARY ACTIONS

The linnorm can take 3 legendary actions, choosing from the options below. Only one legendary action option can be used at a time and only at the end of another creature's turn. The linnorm regains spent legendary actions at the start of its turn.

Detect. The linnorm makes a Wisdom (Perception) check.

Claw Attack. The linnorm makes a claw attack.

Drag (Costs 2 Actions). The linnorm uses Constrict. The linnorm can then swim up to half its swimming speed.

LINNORM, MIDGARD SERPENT

The Midgard Serpent is the greatest of linnorms, the unbounded spawn of a treacherous godling and his monstrous bride. Cast into the sea by the gods when it and its monstrous siblings were discovered, this beast is fated to one day devour the mightiest of the gods. The Midgard Serpent's appetite is endless, as it gorges itself for weeks at a time before descending into the deepest depths of the ocean to drift in the inky depths for years or decades at a time before rising once more to feast. Also called Jormungandr, the Midgard Serpent is over 500 feet long and weighs over 20,000 tons.

Legendary Destroyer. The Midgard Serpent is a solitary beast, tolerating no rivals in the deep waters where it swims. It preys upon ordinary aquatic animals like whales and squid, but also happily devours dragon turtles, krakens, and lesser linnorms, and can depopulate entire cities of aquatic races like sahuagin and merfolk. When it roams close to the surface, storms follow in its wake, and ships are shattered with ease beneath its coils as their crews are devoured. On rare occasions it ventures near to shore, usually when pursuing a ship fleeing before it, and may devastate coastal communities with its onslaught as the storm-tossed sea rises up around it, but it soon retreats to the deep oceans it favors.

God-Eater. The Midgard Serpent is a unique creature, though kin to other great monsters like Fenris Wolf sired by the same forbidden liaisons that gave birth to it. Cast into the sea by the gods long ago, the Midgard Serpent still holds great enmity toward them and their servants, and seeks out divine servants to devour with especial relish. If he chances upon shrines to the gods, he always takes the time to demolish, despoil, and pollute them, vomiting forth his vile and corrupted poisons into the ruins left behind. Jormungandr is not particular in his hatred of the gods, and is equally happy to destroy spaces both sacred and profane. He is a devourer of both magic as well as flesh, consuming the latent magical energies of the world and drawing in the life-giving essence of the universe with every breath. His presence disrupts natural weather and brings with it disastrous storms and a dimming of the light of the world. He is a creature of pure hate, looking always towards that far-off day when the world draws down to its bitter, frozen ending and he and the other great beasts of the world rise up and devour the gods who once cast them down.

LINNORM, MIDGARD SERPENT

Gargantuan dragon (titan), unaligned

Armor Class 19 (natural armor)

Hit Points 553 (27d20+270)

Speed swim 100 ft.

STR	DEX	CON	INT	WIS	CHA
30 (+10)	16 (+3)	30 (+10)	3 (–4)	24 (+7)	29 (+9)

Saving Throws Cha +18, Con +19, Str +19

Skills Athletics +19, Perception +16

Damage Resistances lightning, fire, necrotic, thunder; bludgeoning, piercing, and slashing from nonmagical attacks

Damage Immunities acid, cold

Condition Immunities charmed, frightened, paralyzed

Senses darkvision 120 ft., passive Perception 26

Languages Aquan, Giant (can't speak)

Challenge 30 (155,000 XP)

Innate Spellcasting. The Midgard Serpent's spellcasting ability is Charisma (spell save DC 26). It can innately cast the following spells, requiring no material components:

At will: *freedom of movement, true seeing*

3/day each: *control weather, fog cloud*

1/day each: *earthquake, tsunami*

Legendary Resistance (3/Day). If the Midgard Serpent fails a saving throw, it can choose to succeed instead.

Massive Size. The Midgard Serpent occupies a space of 60 feet by 60 feet instead of the space a Gargantuan creature would normally occupy.

Siege Monster. The Midgard Serpent deals double damage to objects and structures.

Solid Fog. Whenever the Midgard Serpent casts *fog cloud*, the area that the spell occupies is also considered difficult terrain. All melee weapon attack rolls within this area are made with disadvantage, except for the Midgard Serpent's attacks. Ranged weapon attacks simply fail within this area, as the fog is far too thick to have projectiles make it through.

Water Breathing. The Midgard Serpent can only breathe underwater.

ACTIONS

Multiattack. The Midgard Serpent makes one bite attack and one tail attack.

Bite. *Melee Weapon Attack.* +19 to hit, 60 ft. reach, all targets in a 10-foot square. *Hit:* 75 (10d12 + 10) bludgeoning damage plus 65 (10d12) poison damage.

Tail. *Melee Weapon Attack.* +19 to hit, 60 ft. reach, all targets within reach. *Hit:* 43 (6d10 + 10) piercing damage. The Midgard Serpent can choose to grapple one creature it hits instead of dealing damage (escape DC 23).

LEGENDARY ACTIONS

The Midgard Serpent can take 3 legendary actions, choosing from the options below. Only one legendary action option can be used at a time and only at the end of another creature's turn. The Midgard Serpent regains spent legendary actions at the start of its turn.

Charming Gaze (Costs 2 Actions). The Midgard Serpent can focus its gaze on one creature which must succeed a DC 23

Wisdom saving throw or become charmed by the Midgard Serpent. A charmed creature can attempt a saving throw at the end of each of its turns to end the condition.

God-Eater. The Midgard Serpent learns the location of all celestials and fiends as well as clerics and paladins who gain their power from a deity within 60 feet of it. It may immediately make a bite attack against one such creature if there is one within range.

Unnerving Aura. All creatures within 60 feet of the Midgard Serpent must succeed a DC 23 Wisdom saving throw or become frightened of the Midgard Serpent. A frightened creature can attempt a saving throw at the end of each of its turns to end the condition.

LAIR ACTIONS

On initiative count 20 (losing initiative ties), the Midgard Serpent takes a lair action to cause one of the following effects; The Midgard Serpent can't use the same effect two rounds in a row:

• A Midgard Serpent can summon one creature that swims and breathes water of CR 2 or less to a space within 60 feet of it. This creature is loyal to the Midgard Serpent and will do anything to defend it.

• The Midgard Serpent can cause a 10-foot-radius square of water within 60 feet to superheat. Any creatures in those squares must succeed a DC 23 Constitution saving throw or take 7 (2d6) fire damage.

• The Midgard Serpent can cause a 10-foot-radius whirlpool to form in a space within 60 feet of it. All creatures within this area must succeed a DC 23 Dexterity saving throw or be restrained for 1 round.

REGIONAL EFFECTS

The region containing the Midgard Serpent's lair is shaped by its titanic power, which creates one or more of the following effects:

• Underwater lightning storms become frequent, with electricity occasionally arcing through the sea floor and hotspots of boiling water becoming commonplace

• Religious symbols become hot to the touch, almost becoming unbearable to wield within 1 mile of the Midgard Serpent's lair.

The lighting within 1 mile of the Midgard Serpent's lair becomes dim lighting that is impossible to brighten. The area within 150 feet of the Midgard Serpent's lair is darkness that is impossible to brighten.

LIVING ISLAND

Living islands are rare flora found only on Orbis Aurea. They migrate ceaselessly through the ice-locked oceans and arctic plains of their planet, but no one is sure why. Gentle in disposition, bearers of bounty and breakers of otherwise impassable ice, living islands are regarded with reverence and respect by native okanta and giant traditions. Humanoid communities have clustered around living islands since the ancient past, and they have borne gardens, homes, and shrines. Giant legends speak of cities built on the backs of living islands far vaster than any known today, buildings built of bark nestled amidst an overgrown jungle.

Biomass. The main body of a living island is a massive, gradually curved leaf-like growth. Detritus gathers in the bowl of the leaf and is supplemented by complex biological processes, together creating an organic landscape of fertile soil and hardened bark. The living island populates the landscape through gathering other plants and spending long periods of dormancy in areas of abundant flora and wildlife. Below the leaf are its thick, prehensile roots. When still these roots retreat beneath the leaf, but when the living island takes actions these roots spread out to grip the terrain or propel it through the ocean.

LIVING ISLAND

Gargantuan plant, unaligned

Armor Class 19 (natural armour)

Hit Points 396 (24d20+144)

Speed 10 ft., swim 40 ft.

STR	DEX	CON	INT	WIS	CHA
20 (+5)	18 (+4)	22 (+6)	2 (-4)	10 (+0)	7 (-2)

Saving Throws Str +11, Con +12, Wis +6, Cha +4

Skills Athletics +11, Perception +6, Stealth +10

Damage Resistances acid, lightning, radiant; bludgeoning, piercing, and slashing from nonmagical attacks

Damage Immunities cold, poison

Condition Immunities charmed, frightened, paralysed, poisoned

Senses blindsight 120 ft., passive Perception 16

Languages -

Challenge 20 (25,000 XP)

Blend. When the living island remains still, it blends into its terrain and appears to be an island (or small hill). To recognize the living island for what it is a creature must succeed on a DC 22 Wisdom (Survival) check.

Defensive. When a creature hits the living island with a melee attack the island will attempt to force the blow back onto the creature. The creature must succeed on a DC 20 Strength saving throw or have its weapon come flying back at its face, with the creature taking the damage from the melee attack instead of the island.

Growth. Living islands produce enough fruit each day to feed 5 (2d4) Medium creatures. Some of this fruit contains seeds that cause new living islands to grow, usually inside the unfortunate creature. To determine which fruits contain these seeds, a creature must pass a DC 22 Wisdom (Survival) check. If the creature is aware of what a living island is, and is proficient in Wisdom (Survival), it gains advantage on this check. If the check is failed and the fruit is consumed by a living creature (or, subject to GM's discretion, an undead creature wherein it could grow), a living island seed is ingested. The target creature must succeed on a special death saving throw every morning after ingestion, regardless of hit points. These special death saving throws are independent of other death saving throws and do not count towards the tallying of successes or failures when a creature with an ingested seed is reduced to 0 hit points. After three successes, the seed is passed and there are no further ongoing effects. On the first failure, the target gains one level of exhaustion. On the second failure the target gains one level of exhaustion and is poisoned. On the third failure the creature dies and a small miniature island grows from their corpse. Exhaustion levels gained and the poisoned condition inflicted by ingestion of living island seeds may not be cured until the seed is passed. The seeds and their effects can be identified with a DC 20 Wisdom (Medicine) check after ingestion. Once identified, the seeds can be removed with relative ease and a DC 18 Wisdom (Medicine) check, though this is not without risk. Failure results in the creature making an additional special death saving throw as if it were a new day, as the seeds hasten their growth when agitated.

Extra Gargantuan. A living island can be a multitude of sizes, with the average isle being roughly circular with a diameter of 200 ft.

Icebreaker. The living island easily plows through ice and snow, even breaking through the solid sheets of Orbis Aurea's frozen oceans. It can break through solid ice with no difficulty and is not impeded by all but the most extreme forms of difficult terrain.

Thorny Entanglement. During dangerous situations the foliage on the living island acts to protect itself. During combat, the entire island is considered difficult terrain. In addition, each creature on the living island must succeed on a DC 19 Strength saving throw at the start of its turn or become restrained. A creature can use its action to make a DC 19 Strength check, freeing itself or another entangled creature within reach on a success. Creatures restrained by this ability take 13 (3d8) piercing damage at the start of the living island's turn, and an attempt to free another restrained creature is also risky: Regardless of success or failure, the creature attempting to free another takes 13 (3d8) piercing damage on completion of the attempt.

ACTIONS

Multiattack. The living island makes four attacks with its roots.

Roots. *Melee Weapon Attack:* +11 to hit, reach 200 ft., one target. *Hit:* 18 (3d8 + 5) bludgeoning damage.

LORAN

Lorans claim both the ancient patrons deities of the sea and the genie race of marids as their progenitors. When these protean creators foresaw a need for disciplined, loyal aquatic allies, they enlisted genie and elemental-touched mortal volunteers to help shape a new race of agents to guard against the return of their dark and destructive powers of the sea. Lorans appear as beautiful humanoids, though reserved in their demeanor.

Guardians of Ancient Knowledge. While not every loran chooses to pursue a monastic lifestyle, many have endured centuries guarding the memories and relics of the Patrons since the disappearance of the old races and often the cataclysmic devastation of their worlds thereafter. Their discipline as unyielding as the coral ruins they live in, their mission controlled their culture, including career, lifespan, mating, and reproduction. They meditated on the history and teachings of their immortal patrons, passing principles down from generation to generation. They also maintained constant readiness from outside threats, knowing one day an enemy would come to shatter their walls and lives in search of domination.

Loran Monk

Medium humanoid (loran), lawful neutral

Armor Class 16

Hit Points 115 (21d8 + 21)

Speed 40 ft., swim 40 ft.

STR	DEX	CON	INT	WIS	CHA
18 (+4)	17 (+3)	13 (+1)	11 (+0)	14 (+2)	10 (+0)

Saving Throws The loran monk has advantage on saving throws against enchantment spells

Skills Acrobatics +6, Insight +5, Perception +5

Damage Resistance cold

Senses darkvision 60 ft.; passive Perception 15

Languages Aquan, Common

Challenge 5 (1,800 XP)

Amphibious. The loran monk can breathe air and water.

Evasion. If the loran monk is subjected to an effect that allows it to make a Dexterity saving throw to take only half damage, the loran monk instead takes no damage if it succeeds on the saving throw, and only half damage if it fails.

Actions

Multiattack. The loran monk makes three unarmed strikes or three dart attacks.

Unarmed Strike. Melee Weapon Attack: +7 to hit, reach 5 ft., one target. *Hit:* 7 (1d8 + 3) bludgeoning damage. If the target is a creature, the target must succeed on a DC 15 Constitution saving throw or be stunned until the end of the loran monk's next turn.

Dart. Ranged Weapon Attack: +6 to hit, range 20/60 ft., one target. *Hit:* 5 (1d4+3) piercing damage.

Loran Traits

Lorans are defined by their class levels. All lorans have the following racial traits, which you can apply to create a loran NPC.

Ability Score Increase. You gain +2 to Wisdom.

Size. Your size is medium.

Speed. Your base land speed is 30 feet and you have a swim speed of 40 feet.

Darkvision. You can see in the dark up to 60 feet.

Deep Ones. You are resistant to cold damage.

Elemental Affinity. Loran spellcasters you have an affinity for water-based spells. The DC of such spells is increased by 1.

Amphibious. You can breathe both water and air.

Languages. You can speak read and write Aquan and Common.

Loran Monastic Training. Your people have a monastic tradition and you have been trained in basic martial art techniques. Your base AC is 11.

LYCANTHROPE, WERESHARK

In either humanoid or hybrid form, a wereshark is generally burly, has a mouth full of unusually large teeth, and typically has a personality that is both crude and bullying. They're bloodthirsty and are very easy to anger. They will jump into fights they have no stake in just to snap bones and draw blood.

Weresharks prefer life at sea or in port settlements commonly frequented by seagoing merchants and pirates. They can be found leading pirate gangs or loitering at seaside taverns accompanied by crowds of toadies. Since they get into fights so often, they try to stick close to the sea so they can escape into the water if they bite off more than they can chew. The other members of a wereshark's crew learn quickly that the boss is bound to skip out without much notice once a bigger fish comes along.

WERESHARK

Medium humanoid (human, shapechanger), chaotic evil

Armor Class 11 in humanoid form, 13 (natural armor) in shark or hybrid form

Hit Points 90 (12d8+36)

Speed 30 ft., swim 40 ft. (in shark form only)

STR	DEX	CON	INT	WIS	CHA
18 (+4)	13 (+1)	17 (+3)	10 (+0)	13 (+1)	10 (+0)

Skills Perception +7, Stealth +7

Damage Immunities bludgeoning, piercing, and slashing from nonmagical attacks not made with silvered weapons

Senses blindsense 30 ft. (shark or hybrid form only); passive Perception 17

Languages Common (can't speak in shark form)

Challenge 6 (2,300 XP)

Amphibious. The wereshark can breathe air or water.

Blood Frenzy. The wereshark has advantage on melee attack rolls against any creature that doesn't have all its hit points.

Shapechanger. The wereshark can use its action to polymorph into a shark-humanoid hybrid or into a hunter shark, or back into its true form, which is humanoid. Its statistics, other than its AC, and its size, are the same in each form. Any equipment it is wearing or carrying isn't transformed. It reverts to its true form if it dies.

ACTIONS

Multiattack (hybrid form only). In humanoid form, the wereshark makes two trident attacks. In hybrid form, it can substitute a bite for one *Melee Weapon Attack.*

Bite (Shark or Hybrid Form only). *Melee Weapon Attack:* +7 to hit, reach 5 ft., one target. *Hit:* 13 (2d8 + 4) piercing damage. If the target is a humanoid, it must succeed on a DC 14 Constitution saving throw or be cursed with wereshark lycanthropy.

Trident (Humanoid or Hyrbid Form Only). *Melee or Ranged Weapon Attack:* +7 to hit, reach 5 ft. or range 20/60 ft., one creature. *Hit:* 7 (1d6 + 4) piercing damage, or 8 (1d8 + 4) piercing damage if used with two hands to make a melee attack.

MERFOLK

Merfolk guardians are the chosen of nature and its divine protectors. They are more mystical than other merfolk, and also more savage, mysterious, and close to nature. Sometimes, they live among other merfolk as special protectors, but there are entire tribes of merfolk guardians as well. Tribes of these merfolk seem forbidding even to other merfolk.

Merfolk Guardian

Medium humanoid (merfolk), neutral

Armor Class 11

Hit Points 44 (8d8+8)

Speed 10 ft., swim 40 ft.

STR	DEX	CON	INT	WIS	CHA
14 (+2)	13 (+1)	12 (+1)	11 (+0)	11 (+0)	12 (+1)

Skills Perception +3

Senses passive Perception 13

Languages Aquan, Common

Challenge 1/2 (100 XP)

Amphibious. The merfolk can breathe air and water.

Aquatic Telepathy. The merfolk can communicate with aquatic beasts within 100 feet using telepathy. The merfolk can comprehend and verbally communicate with aquatic beasts. The knowledge and awareness of many beasts is limited by their intelligence, but at minimum, beasts can give information about nearby locations and monsters, including whatever they can perceive or have perceived within the past day.

Eel Strike. When the merfolk takes the Disengage action, it may make a single weapon attack as a bonus action at any time during its turn.

Innate Spellcasting. The merfolk's innate spellcasting ability is Charisma (spell save DC 11). It can innately cast the following spells, requiring no material components.

1/day: *animal friendship*, *dominate beast* (aquatic beasts only), *hold monster* (aquatic beasts only), *message*, *sending* (only through water)

Actions

Multiattack. The merfolk makes two spear attacks.

Spear. Melee or Ranged Weapon Attack: +4 to hit, reach 5 ft. or range 20/60 ft., one target. *Hit:* 5 (1d6 + 2) piercing damage, or 6 (1d8 + 2) piercing damage if used with two hands to make a melee attack.

Share Breath. The merfolk touches one creature, and that creatures magically gains the Amphibious feature for 10 minutes.

NEREID

Nereids are capricious and often dangerous aquatic fey that appear as strikingly beautiful women, often seen bathing unclothed in the water. Many sailors have met their doom following a nereid, for though a nereid's beauty is otherworldly, her watery kiss is death. Others seek out nereids, for if one can secure control over the creature's shawl, the cloth can be used to force the nereid's compliance. A nereid forced to obey in this manner immediately attempts to slay her master as soon as she can secure her shawl's safety.

Sea Friends. Nereids are sometimes accompanied by a friendly aquatic predator like a shark, giant eel, or giant squid.

Nereid

Medium fey, chaotic neutral

Armor Class 19

Hit Points 120 (12d8+48)

Speed 30 ft., swim 60 ft.

STR	DEX	CON	INT	WIS	CHA
11 (+0)	21 (+5)	19 (+4)	14 (+2)	18 (+4)	18 (+4)

Skills Nature+5, Perception +7, Performance +10

Senses darkvision 60 ft.; passive Perception 17

Languages Aquan, Common, Sylvan

Challenge 7 (2,900 XP)

Innate Spellcasting. The nereid's innate spellcasting ability is Wisdom (spell save DC 15). The nereid can innately cast the following spells, requiring no material components:

At will: *control water*

Magic Resistance. The nereid has advantage on saving throws against spells and other magical effects.

Shawl. A nereid's shawl (6 hit points) contains a portion of her life force. If the shawl is ever destroyed, the nereid takes 1d6 necrotic damage per hour until she dies. A nereid can craft a new shawl from water by making a DC 10 Wisdom check, but each attempt takes 1d4 hours to complete.

Transparency. When underwater, a nereid's body becomes transparent, effectively rendering her invisible. She can become visible or transparent on her turn without using an action.

Unarmored Defense. If she wears no armor, a nereid's Armor Class equals 10 + her Dexterity modifier + her Charisma modifier.

Actions

Multiattack. The nereid uses Beguile, then Suggestion.

Blind. Ranged Weapon Attack: +8 to hit, range 30/60 ft., one target. *Hit:* the target must make a DC 15 Constitution saving throw. On a failure, the target is poisoned for 1 minute. A target is blinded while poisoned. At the end of each of its turns, the target can make another Constitution saving throw. On a success, the target is no longer poisoned.

Beguile. Any creature within 30 feet of the nereid must make a DC 15 Wisdom saving throw. If failed, they have disadvantage on Wisdom (Perception) checks to perceive any creature other than the nereid. Creatures in combat with the nereid have advantage on this saving throw, and creatures that can't be charmed are immune. The effect ends if the nereid is incapacitated or cannot be seen.

Drowning Kiss. A nereid can flood the lungs of one target within 5 feet that is willing, incapacitated, or affected by her Beguile. She touches the target, traditionally by kissing the creature on the lips. The target must make a DC 15 Constitution saving throw or immediately begin drowning. Drowning creatures begin choking. At the end of each of its turns, the target can make another Constitution saving throw. On a success, the target is no longer drowning.

Suggestion. The nereid suggests an action to a creature she can see within 30 feet that can hear and understand her. If the target fails a DC 15 Wisdom saving throw, it pursues the suggested course of action to the best of its ability. The effect ends when the action is completed, after 8 hours, or if the creature is harmed by the nereid or her allies, whichever comes first. Self-destructive suggestions are ignored, and creatures that can't be charmed are immune.

SAHUAGIN, SELACHIM

The unpredictability and viciousness of the sahuagin race isn't just an aspect of their sharklike temperament—it seems to be inherent in their very beings. The unusual and typically deadly mutants common to the race attest to this, their forms altering and becoming more deadly based either on the needs of the community or ambiguous environmental factors. Whatever the case, sahuagin mutants often rise to positions of respect and influence in sahuagin communities, their innate advantages instantly placing them among their people's rulers. Of these mutants, four-armed sahuagin brutes and malenti—sahuagin with the appearances of sea elves—arise most commonly, though these are in no way the only sahuagin mutants known to the savage seas.

Spontaneous Mutation. While the more common mutants among sahuagin have mutated into a specific form, the subspecies known as the selachim have inherited a uniquely protean gift of triggering a variety of mutations to suit the tactical needs of its mission.

SAHUAGIN SELACHIM

Medium humanoid (sahuagin), lawful evil

Armor Class 13 (natural armor)

Hit Points 84 (13d8+26)

Speed 30 ft., swim 60 ft.

STR	DEX	CON	INT	WIS	CHA
16 (+3)	13 (+1)	14 (+2)	14 (+2)	13 (+1)	10 (+0)

Saving Throws Int +4, Str +4

Skills Athletics +6, Perception +3

Senses blindsight 30 ft., darkvision 60 ft., passive Perception 13

Languages Sahuagin

Challenge 3 (700 XP)

Blood Frenzy. The sahuagin mutant has advantage on melee attack rolls against any creature that doesn't have all its hit points.

Limited Amphibiousness. The sahuagin mutant can breathe air and water, but it needs to be submerged at least once every 4 hours to avoid suffocating.

Shark Telepathy. The sahuagin mutant can magically command any shark within 120 feet of it, using a limited telepathy.

ACTIONS

Multiattack. The sahuagin mutant makes one bite attack and two claw attacks.

Bite. *Melee Weapon Attack.* +5 to hit, 5 ft. reach, one target. *Hit:* 7 (1d8 + 3) piercing damage.

Claw. *Melee Weapon Attack.* +5 to hit, 5 ft. reach, one target. *Hit:* 7 (1d8 + 3) slashing damage.

Spontaneous Mutation. A sahuagin mutant can tap into the latent mutational potential of its species, granting it one of the following mutational benefits for 1 minute. Once it uses this ability, it cannot use it again until it completes a short rest. Alternatively, it may choose to gain one of the following mutational benefits for 1 hour; if it does so, it cannot use this ability again until it completes a long rest.

- *Angler:* The sahuagin mutant's skin becomes pallid and eyeless. Its blindsight increases to 90 feet. A glowing tendril protruding from its head a sightless sahuagin causes all sighted creatures within 10 feet to have disadvantage on melee attack rolls against the sahuagin mutant.

- *Primordial:* The sahuagin mutant's size increases to Large and its Armor Class also increases to 15.

- *Spinefish:* The sahuagin mutant's flesh becomes covered with hundreds of needle-like spines. Creatures that grapple or are grappled by the sahuagin, or hit it with an unarmed strike take 3 (1d6) points of piercing damage.

- *Thresher:* The sahuagin mutant's maw expands and fills with rows of shark-like teeth, while its lower body becomes shark-like, resembling a monstrous merfolk. Its land speed is decreased to 5 feet but its swim speed increased to 80 feet.

SARGASSUM FIEND

A sargassum fiend is a free-floating mass of intelligent seaweed capable of luring its victims to their deaths via a powerful hallucinogenic pheromone. Once the sargassum fiend lures prey within striking distance, it grabs the entranced creature and attempts to crush it to death. Experienced sailors tell tales of entire crews jumping overboard to swim out to a murderous field of the sea plants. Sargassum fiends usually reach sizes up to 10 feet in diameter before splitting, their means of asexual reproduction. Mutations have been known to exist, however, and sea-faring scholars have recorded individual sargassum fiends reaching masses of truly enormous size.

Sargassum Fiend

Large plant, unaligned

Armor Class 16 (natural armor)

Hit Points 136 (13d10+65)

Speed 20 ft., climb 20 ft., swim 40 ft.

STR	DEX	CON	INT	WIS	CHA
25 (+7)	14 (+2)	20 (+5)	2 (−4)	11 (+0)	15 (+2)

Saving Throws Con +9, Str +11

Skills Perception +8

Damage Resistances bludgeoning, cold, piercing

Senses blindsight 60 ft., tremorsense 60 ft., passive Perception 18

Languages Deep Speech, telepathy 120 ft.

Challenge 9 (5,000 XP)

Mirage. A sargassum fiend emits a powerful scent that causes specific, miragelike hallucinations. All creatures within 300 feet of a sargassum fiend must make a DC 16 Wisdom saving throw or become charmed by the scent. A charmed creature sees the sargassum fiend as whatever would most compel it to approach. This might be a lost loved one, a child in need of help, an enchanting mermaid, the promise of dry land, and so on. This effect ends immediately if the sargassum fiend makes an attack against any target.

Water Breathing. The sargassum fiend can only breathe underwater.

Actions

Multiattack. The sargassum fiend makes two slam attacks.

Slam. *Melee Weapon Attack.* +11 to hit, 10 ft. reach, one target. *Hit:* 29 (4d10 + 7) bludgeoning damage. Instead of dealing damage, the sargassum fiend can grapple the target (escape DC 16).

SCYLLA

The scylla is one of the more nightmarish aberrations to blight the mortal world, horrifying creatures with the upper body of a beautiful woman but a lower body of snapping wolf or serpent heads and writhing tentacles. Conflicting tales of her origins abound, from demonic flesh-crafting and arcane experiments to a divine curse handed down by a vengeful deity. The most popular stories cast the first scylla as the monstrous spawn of a union between a mortal and a god. Whatever the case, scyllas are fortunately quite rare, enough so that many consider them nothing more than tall tales told by sailors deep in their cups.

Ship-Hunter. Scyllas dwell along major shipping lanes, often near coastlines, where they use their spells to lure entire ships to their doom. The hideous monsters are intelligent creatures, though half-mad with hunger and self-loathing. They normally do not use weapons, but when they do, they prefer to fight with light weapons wielded by their human-sized upper arms. However, they much prefer to keep their hands free to utilize magic items like wands, staves, and other powerful devices.

Scylla

Huge aberration, chaotic evil

Armor Class 18 (natural armor)

Hit Points 507 (35d12+280)

Speed 30 ft., swim 50 ft.

STR	DEX	CON	INT	WIS	CHA
24 (+7)	29 (+9)	27 (+8)	16 (+3)	23 (+6)	22 (+6)

Saving Throws Dex +16, Con +15, Cha +13

Skills Acrobatics +16, Deception +20, Insight +13, Intimidation +13, Perception +13

Damage Resistances fire; bludgeoning, piercing, and slashing from nonmagical attacks

Condition Immunities charmed, prone

Senses truesight 60 ft., blindsight 200 ft., passive Perception 23

Languages Abyssal, Aquan, Common

Challenge 23 (62,000 XP)

Amphibious. The scylla can breathe water and air.

Innate Spellcasting. The scylla's spellcasting ability is Wisdom (spell save DC 21). It can innately cast the following spells, requiring no material components:

At will: *acid arrow, control water, fog cloud*

3/day each: *dispel magic, major image*

Legendary Resistance (3/day). If the Scylla fails a saving throw, it can choose to succeed instead.

Magic Resistance. The scylla has advantage on saving throws against spells and other magical effects.

Multi-Headed. While the scylla can see in all directions, and has advantage on Wisdom (Perception) checks, which applies to its passive Perception score. It also has advantage on saving throws against being blinded, deafened, stunned, and knocked unconscious.

Actions

Multiattack. The scylla can use its frightful presence. It then makes three bite or tentacle attacks. In humanoid form, it may instead make three weapon attacks.

Bite. *Melee Weapon Attack:* +14 to hit, reach 15 ft., one grappled target. *Hit:* 25 (4d8 + 7) piercing damage, and 18 (4d8) necrotic damage, and the target can't regain hit points until the end of its next turn.

Tentacle. *Melee Weapon Attack:* +14 to hit, reach 15 ft., one target. *Hit:* 29 (4d10 + 7) bludgeoning damage, and the target is grappled (escape DC 22). Until this grapple ends, the target is restrained. The scylla has eight tentacles, each of which can grapple one target.

Poisoned Dagger (humanoid form only). *Melee or Ranged Weapon Attack:* +16 to hit, reach 5 ft. or range 20/60 ft., one creature. *Hit:* 9 (1d4 + 7) piercing damage, and 18 (4d8) poison damage.

Frightful Presence. Each creature of the scylla's choice that is within 100 feet of the scylla and aware of it must succeed on a DC 21 Wisdom saving throw or become frightened for 1 minute. A creature can repeat the saving throw at the end of each of its turns, ending the effect on itself on a success. If a creature's saving throw is successful or the effect ends for it, the creature is immune to the scylla's Frightful Presence for the next 24 hours.

Change Shape. The scylla magically polymorphs into a Small or Medium female humanoid, or back into her true form. The scylla loses its bite and tentacle attacks but can wield weapons or make slam attacks as appropriate for its form. Its statistics are otherwise the same in each form. Any equipment it is wearing or carrying isn't transformed. She reverts to her true form if she dies.

Legendary Actions

The scylla can take 2 legendary actions, choosing from the options below. Only one legendary action option can be used at a time and only at the end of another creature's turn. The scylla regains spent legendary actions at the start of its turn.

Tentacle. The scylla makes one attack with its tentacle.

Bite (Costs 2 actions). The scylla makes one attack with its bite.

Spell (Costs 2 actions). The scylla uses one of its spells.

SEA BONZE

Sea bonzes are formed from the combined despair and horror of death at sea, such as when a ship sinks and its entire crew drowns. No single restless soul empowers a sea bonze—it combines the anger and doom of all who die in such close proximity. Reawakened as mammoth ship-wreckers, these angry spirits have no memory of their past lives and seek to inflict the doom they suffered on others who ply the seas. Their hatred does not make them mindless, however, and more than one lucky crew member has talked her entire ship's way out of total annihilation. Sea bonzes have an unusual respect for those with wit and guile and sometimes consider sparing those they deem worthy of their esteem. Those who try to defend themselves with brawn and weapons, however, receive no mercy from the enormous monsters.

Nothing but Death. A sea bonze's body is black and leathery like that of a squid when seen up close, but an ever-present mist clings to it even in the water, causing it to appear at first glance to be made out of the black waters of the ocean itself, or a bank of shadow and fog rising up from the waves. The entire creature is featureless and smooth, making its empty visage and its two gleaming pinpricks of light for eyes all the more horrifying.

Sea Bonze

Gargantuan undead, neutral evil

Armor Class 19 (natural armor)

Hit Points 280 (16d20+112)

Speed 40 ft., swim 80 ft.

STR	DEX	CON	INT	WIS	CHA
18 (+4)	28 (+9)	25 (+7)	16 (+3)	18 (+4)	24 (+7)

Saving Throws Con +12, Int +10, Wis +9

Damage Resistance acid, fire; bludgeoning, piercing, and slashing from nonmagical attacks

Damage Immunities cold, lightning

Condition Immunities charmed, frightened

Skills Intimidation +13, Perception +10

Senses blindsight 120 ft., darkvision 120 ft., passive Perception 20

Languages Aquan, Common

Challenge 19 (22,000 XP)

Innate Spellcasting. A sea bonze's spellcasting ability is Charisma (spell save DC 21). It can innately cast the following spells, requiring no material components:

3/day: *antilife shell, control water*

1/day each: *control weather, storm of vengeance*

Untraceable. The sea bonze is immune to all spells and effects made to learn its location or gain information about it.

Actions

Multiattack. The sea bonze makes two slam attacks.

Slam. *Melee Weapon Attack.* +10 to hit, 20 ft. reach, one target. *Hit:* 59 (10d10 + 4) bludgeoning damage.

Dooming Gaze. A sea bonze can gaze at one creature within 120 feet and attempt to overwhelm its mind with fear. That creature must succeed a DC 19 Wisdom saving throw or be paralyzed. A paralyzed creature can attempt another saving throw at the end of each of its turns to end this effect. Once a creature that was paralyzed breaks free from that condition, they must attempt another DC 19 Wisdom saving throw or become frightened of the sea bonze. A frightened creature can attempt another saving throw at the end of each of its turns to end this effect. A creature that is immune to the frightened condition is immune to both effects of this ability.

Draining Strike (3/day). *Melee Weapon Attack.* +10 to hit, 20 ft. reach, one target. *Hit:* 117 (18d12) necrotic damage plus the target must succeed a DC 19 Constitution saving throw or gain 1 negative level.

Elusive (1/day). A sea bonze has long been the stuff of maritime legends, but despite countless attempts to hunt them, they are rarely encountered unless they wish it. While in water, the sea bonze can move up to 400 feet in a single movement without leaving any trace of its passing (while under the effects of a *pass without trace* spell). The sea bonze gains advantage to its Dexterity (Stealth) ability checks while making this movement.

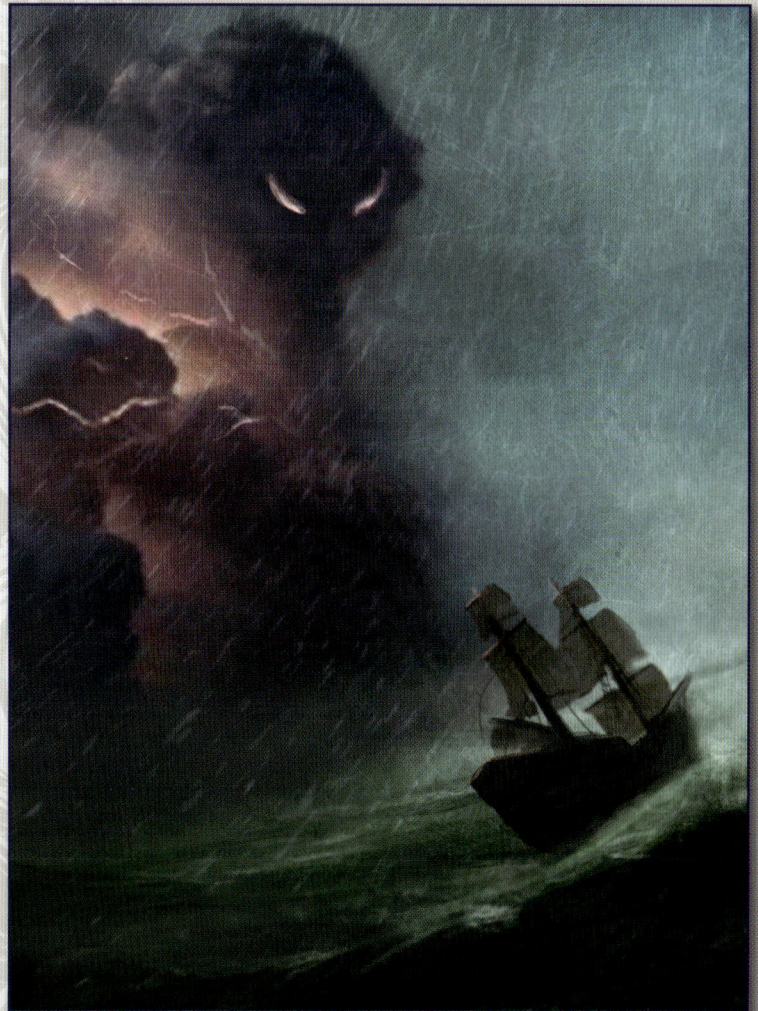

SEA SERPENT

Tales of immense sea serpents have colored the accounts of seagoing folk since the first ship sailed beyond sight of land. Yet proof of these immense and elusive creatures is remarkably difficult to come by, for not only is the ocean vast and the true sea serpent rare, but these creatures are quite adept at both avoiding capture and destroying ships bent on such a daunting task. Due to the sea serpent's hermitic nature, many sailors take to ascribing the sighting of such a beast to an omen, although whether the sighting portends peril or providence depends as much upon the ship's morale as it does anything else—the sea serpent itself has little interest in prophecy, and only its hunger determines how dangerous its proximity to a curious ship can be. Deadly danger surely awaits, however, when its spine-frilled neck arches up from the water like a snake ready to strike.

Sea Serpent

Gargantuan beast, unaligned

Armor Class 16 (natural armor)

Hit Points 217 (15d20 + 60)

Speed 20 ft., swim 60 ft.

STR	DEX	CON	INT	WIS	CHA
24 (+7)	14 (+2)	19 (+4)	3 (-4)	11 (+0)	11 (+0)

Saving Throws Str +11, Con +8

Skills Perception +4, Stealth +6

Damage Resistances fire

Damage Immunities cold

Senses darkvision 120 ft., passive Perception 14

Languages -

Challenge 12 (8,400 XP)

Elusive. When not in combat, a sea serpent cannot be detected by divination magic or seen through scrying.

Legendary Resistance (1/Day). If the sea serpent fails a saving throw, it can choose to succeed instead.

Siege Monster. The sea serpent deals double damage to objects and structures.

Water Breathing. The sea serpent can breathe only underwater.

Actions

Multiattack. The sea serpent makes two attacks: once with its bite and once with its constrict.

Bite. *Melee Weapon Attack:* +11 to hit, reach 20 ft., one target. *Hit:* 25 (4d8 + 7) piercing damage.

Constrict. *Melee Weapon Attack:* +11 to hit, reach 20 ft., one target. *Hit:* 21 (4d6 + 7) bludgeoning damage, and the target is grappled (escape DC 21). Until this grapple ends, the creature is restrained, and the sea serpent can't constrict another target.

Elusive Dive. The sea serpent takes the Dash action, and until the beginning of its next turn, it gains a +10 bonus on Dexterity (Stealth) checks and cannot be tracked by nonmagical means.

Legendary Actions

A sea serpent can take 3 legendary actions, choosing from the options below. Only one legendary action option can be used at a time and only at the end of another creature's turn. A sea serpent regains spent legendary actions at the start of its turn.

Detect (Costs 1 Action). The sea serpent makes a Wisdom (Perception) check.

Surge (Costs 1 Action). The sea serpent swims its base movement rate, without provoking opportunity attacks.

Tail Slap (Costs 2 Actions). The sea serpent makes a melee attack: +11 to hit, reach 20 ft., one target. *Hit:* 21 (4d6 + 7) bludgeoning damage, and the target must make a DC 19 Strength saving throw. On a failed save, the target is knocked prone.

SEAWEED SIREN

Seaweed sirens hunt near the shore, where they wait for clam diggers strolling the beaches, lone fisherfolk, or even passing ships. The creature's three singing heads sway atop serpentine necks that extend from a bulbous body split by a wide, toothy mouth. Pungent strands of seaweed cover the creature like slimy hair. Once a seaweed siren spots its prey, the creature lurks just under the water and allows its three strange heads to protrude above the surface. These heads are nothing more than appendages, and while it can breathe through them it doesn't use them to eat. Seaweed sirens' heads grow differently depending on where the creature developed in order to match the skin tone and apparent ethnicity of the surrounding humanoid population. In addition, the heads are eyeless—the siren sees using the many eyes on its main body mass. A seaweed siren stands over 8 feet tall from the tip of its stubby legs to the top of its heads and is nearly 7 feet in diameter. The creature weighs upward of 3,500 pounds.

Horrific Hybrid. At first glance, this creature appears to blur the line between plant and animal. Three eyeless heads sway above the central body mass, constantly singing, chanting, and speaking in nonsense languages and simple babble. Seaweed covers the creature's three false heads and its main central body—a form of camouflage to help the beast remain hidden while hunting. Six stout, crablike legs carry this creature along the coast and through the rocky tide pools it inhabits.

Entrancing Cacophony. The seaweed siren's heads sing songs and babble in strange nonsense languages to fuel the seaweed siren's many special abilities. Even when not in use against a potential meal, the heads seemingly converse with each other, holding lengthy conversations full of random syllables and made-up words. Once it draws its prey near, the seaweed siren attempts to charm or bewilder its foe to gain the advantage. After this, the creature moves closer and begins to devour its still-living victim. While the seaweed siren prefers to dine on living humanoids, it uses its strident squall attacks to incapacitate or kill prey that flees or resists its charm attempts.

Seaweed sirens sometimes ally themselves with other aquatic creatures to share in hunts or for mutual protection. Sahuagin typically don't trust them but may ally with them long enough to capture new slaves and restock their humanoid food supply. Locathah sometimes use these strange beasts as protectors, keeping them well fed in return for the creatures serving as lookouts and sentinels. Merfolk and aquatic elves avoid seaweed sirens, and even go so far as to sometimes warn other humanoid communities when one is discovered to be hunting nearby.

Seaweed sirens use a form of aggressive mimicry, appearing to have humanoid features in order to lure in their preferred meals. They can converse in Aklo, and constantly babbles in glossolalia, but if it manages to talk with another sentient being that has a language long enough, it begins mimicking the other's language and speech patterns, eventually sounding exactly like it. Though a seaweed siren can use its *tongues* spell to understand and speak any language, it prefers to talk with and mimic its conversational partners without resorting to using this ability. Some speculate the creature catalogs every conversation in order to add to the collection of sounds and words that power its cacophony special ability.

SEAWEED SIREN

Large monstrosity, unaligned

Armor Class 18 (natural armor)

Hit Points 294 (28d10+140)

Speed 30 ft., swim 30 ft.

STR	DEX	CON	INT	WIS	CHA
29 (+9)	16 (+3)	20 (+5)	11 (+0)	16 (+3)	21 (+5)

Saving Throws Str +14, Con +15, Wis +13, Cha +13

Skills Athletics +15, Deception +11, Perception +9, Stealth +9

Damage Resistances fire; bludgeoning, piercing, and slashing from nonmagical attacks

Damage Immunities acid, cold

Condition Immunities charmed, frightened

Senses darkvision 120 ft., passive Perception 19

Languages Aklo

Challenge 17 (18,000 XP)

Cacophony. The seaweed siren projects a constant noise that disrupts spellcasting. Any creature casting a spell within 100 feet of the seaweed siren requires a DC 19 Constitution saving throw. Failure means the spell fails to be cast. The action is used, but any spell slots or uses per day are not. In addition, any hearing-based perception checks made within 100 feet of the seaweed siren have disadvantage. The seaweed siren can use its bonus action to stop using this ability, or to reactivate it.

Innate Spellcasting. The seaweed siren's spellcasting ability is Charisma (spell save DC 18). It can innately cast the following spells, requiring no material components:

At will: *suggestion, tongues, minor illusion*

1/day each: *bestow curse, dominate, irresistible dance*

Multi-Headed. While the seaweed siren can see in all directions, and has advantage on Wisdom (Perception) checks, which applies to its passive Perception score. It also has advantage on saving throws against being blinded, deafened, stunned, and knocked unconscious. Whenever the seaweed siren takes 40 or more damage in a single turn, one of its heads dies. If all three heads die, the seaweed siren can no longer use its Cacophony ability, or its innate spellcasting. Heads regrow at a rate of one per day.

Water Breathing. The seaweed siren cannot breathe air. It can move on land but must hold its breath.

ACTIONS

Multiattack. The seaweed siren makes three bite attacks.

Bite. Melee Weapon Attack: +15 to hit, reach 5 ft., one target. *Hit:* 20 (2d10 + 9) piercing damage and 11 (2d10) poison damage.

Sonic Beam (Recharge 4-6). The seaweed siren uses its heads to create a wail that affects everything in a 60-foot line. Each creature in that line must make a DC 18 Constitution saving throw, taking 56 (12d8) thunder damage, or half as much on a successful saving throw. Creatures failing their saving throw are also deafened for 1 hour, or deafened permanently if already deaf.

SELKIE

Selkies are clever and brutal seal-like beings that often inhabit the colder oceans of the world. Although capable predators, selkies are best known for their mysterious shapechanging ability, which allows them to come ashore in the guise of land dwellers and even live among other races before luring their victims beneath the waves to drown. In its natural form, a selkie has webbed, clawed hands and a muscular trunk ending in broad flippers. A selkie's head is a blend of human and seal, with large eyes and a mouth full of curved teeth. Selkies' coats range from chestnut brown to slate, dappled with darker spots of gray. Male selkies grow to a length of 6-1/2 feet but can weigh up to 300 pounds because of the extra fat the creatures need to survive in colder climes. Females are slightly shorter and slimmer. Selkies typically live up to 75 years.

SELKIE

Medium fey, chaotic neutral

Armor Class 15 (natural armor)

Hit Points 143 (22d8 + 44)

Speed 20 ft., 50 ft. swim

STR	DEX	CON	INT	WIS	CHA
18 (+4)	17 (+3)	14 (+2)	13 (+1)	14 (+2)	19 (+4)

Saving Throws Dex +6, Cha +7

Skills Athletics +7, Deception +7, Insight +5, Perception +5, Stealth +6

Damage Resistances cold

Senses darkvision 60 ft., passive Perception 15

Languages Aquan, Common

Challenge 6 (2,300 XP)

Hold Breath. The selkie can hold its breath for 1 hour.

Echo of Reason. The selkie has advantage on its Charisma checks made when talking or singing.

Magic Resistance. The selkie has advantage on saving throws against spells and other magical effects.

Selkie Coat. When a selkie changes shape and goes on land, she leaves behind a sealskin coat among the rocks on the shore. A creature that takes its coat can control the selkie as if it were charmed and the selkie cannot use its Change Shape ability again until it recovers the coat. If the coat is destroyed, it can shed a new sealskin at the next full moon (or after 21 days in the absence of a lunar cycle).

Scent. The selkie has advantage on Perception checks made involving scent. When underwater, it can also track specific scents from up to a mile away.

ACTIONS

Multiattack. The selkie makes two melee attacks, one of which can be its bite if it is in its true form. In seal form, it can make two bite attacks.

Bite (True Form or Seal Form Only). *Melee Weapon Attack:* +7 to hit, reach 5 ft., one target. *Hit:* 9 (1d10+4) piercing damage.

Dagger. *Melee or Ranged Weapon Attack:* +7 to hit, reach 5 ft., one target. *Hit:* 6 (1d4+4) piercing damage.

Claws (True Form or Seal Form Only). *Ranged Weapon Attack:* +7 to hit, reach 5 ft., one target. *Hit:* 8 (1d8+4) slashing damage

Charming Song. The selkie sings a charming song. When it does, it can target one creature, who must make a DC 15 Charisma saving throw. On a failure, the creature is charmed for 1 minute. As a bonus action, the selkie can instruct a charmed creature to use its movement to enter or swim to the center of the nearest body of water, regardless of any danger. Charmed creatures can attempt a new saving throw at the end of each of their turns. If a creature's saving throw is successful, or the effect ends for it, the creature is immune to the selkie's Charming Song for the next 24 hours.

Change Shape. The selkie magically polymorphs into a Small or Medium female humanoid, the shape of a seal, or back into its true form. Its statistics are the same in each form. Any equipment it is wearing or carrying isn't transformed. It reverts to its true form if it dies.

SHARK

The true nightmare of the sea is the megalodon, a shark that represents the pinnacle of this species' evolution. Horrifying in its immense size and ruinous appetite, the megalodon is certainly the beast behind many legends of enormous fish who swallow ships whole. A megalodon is 60 feet long and weighs 100,000 pounds.

MEGALODON SHARK

Gargantuan beast, unaligned

Armor Class 15 (natural armor)

Hit Points 232 (15d20+75)

Speed 0 ft., swim 50 ft.

STR	DEX	CON	INT	WIS	CHA
27 (+8)	14 (+2)	21 (+5)	1 (-5)	12 (+1)	10 (+0)

Saving Throws Wis +5

Skills Perception +5

Senses blindsight 60 ft.; passive Perception 15

Languages -

Challenge 11 (7,200 XP)

Blood Frenzy. The shark has advantage on melee attack rolls against any creature that doesn't have all its hit points.

Water Breathing. The shark can breathe only underwater.

ACTIONS

Bite. *Melee Weapon Attack:* +12 to hit, reach 5 ft., one target. *Hit:* 30 (4d10 + 8) piercing damage, and a Large or smaller target must succeed on a DC 18 Strength saving throw or be swallowed whole. If its bite attack is a critical hit, it can swallow a Huge creature in the same way. A swallowed creature is blinded and restrained and has total cover against attacks and other effects outside the megalodon. It takes 11 (2d10) bludgeoning damage and 11 (2d10) piercing damage at the start of each of the megalodon's turns. A megalodon can have one Huge creature, up to three Large creatures, or up to 10 Medium creatures swallowed at a time. If the megalodon takes 45 damage or more on a single turn from the swallowed creature, the megalodon must succeed on a DC 14 Constitution saving throw at the end of that turn or regurgitate the creature, which falls prone within 5 feet of the shark. If the megalodon dies, a swallowed creature is no longer restrained by it and can escape from the corpse by using 10 feet of movement, exiting prone.

SIREN

These bizarre beings have the bodies of hawks, owls, or eagles, but the heads of beautiful human women. Their faces typically reflect the human ethnicity dominant in the area in which they lair, and they almost always bear a vibrant and youthful countenance. A typical siren has a wingspan of 8 feet and weighs 120 pounds.

Heartbreaker. All sirens are female and long-lived. The oldest known sirens haunt their territories for nearly a millennium, although most only live for a few hundred years. Sirens require male humanoids to mate, and several times per decade either capture or rescue bold or comely sailors who enter their territories. Stories abound of sirens dying—either through heartache or suicide—when sailors they attempted to lure overcame their compelling powers and escaped their grasps. Sirens always live near the sea, where their powerful voices can carry over the waves and attract the attention of unwary sailors who trespass near their isles.

SIREN

Medium monstrosity, chaotic neutral

Armor Class 14

Hit Points 82 (15d8 + 15)

Speed 30 ft., 60 ft. fly

STR	DEX	CON	INT	WIS	CHA
10 (+0)	19 (+4)	12 (+1)	14 (+2)	17 (+3)	18 (+4)

Saving Throws Dex +6

Skills Acrobatics +7, History +5, Insight +6, Perception +6, Performance +10, Stealth +7

Condition Immunities charmed, frightened

Senses darkvision 60 ft., passive Perception 16

Languages Auran, Common

Challenge 3 (700 XP)

ACTIONS

Multiattack. The siren makes two attacks with its talons.

Talons. *Melee Weapon Attack:* +6 to hit, reach 5 ft., one target. *Hit:* 9 (1d10 + 4) slashing damage.

Alluring Voice. When the siren sings, it can cause all creatures within 200 feet of it to make a DC 15 Charisma saving throw. Those that fail are charmed and are compelled to do anything the siren asks. As a bonus action, the siren can either instruct the creatures that it has charmed to take an action, or to stay incapacitated. The siren cannot tell victims to attack their allies. A creature can repeat the saving throw at the end of each of its turns, ending the effect on itself on a success. The effect also ends if the siren moves further than 250 feet from its charmed victim. If a creature's saving throw is successful, or the effect ends for it, the creature is immune to this siren's Song of Charming for the next 24 hours.

Screech (Recharge 5-6). The siren lets loose a shrill shout in a 30-foot cone. Each creature in that area must make a DC 14 Constitution saving throw, taking 17 (5d6) thunder damage on a failed save, or half as much on a successful one.

SLAUGHTERMAW LAMPREY

The slaughtermaw lamprey is a long, scale-less fish that superficially resembles a jawless eel with many rows of barbed teeth and poisonous spines along their tail fins. Slaughtermaw lampreys are well acclimated to the icy waters and crushing depths of the ocean trenches of Orbis Aurea when they are adults, but they have to travel vast distances to create nests for their eggs, which must be laid in the shallow coastal regions to survive. Adult slaughtermaw lampreys remain to protect their eggs, but typically travel back to the depths after their eggs hatch, abandoning their young. After hatching, young slaughtermaw lampreys burrow into the sediments along the coast to filter feed for several months until they enter a metamorphosis to become adults. When the slaughtermaw lampreys finally emerge from their metamorphosis, they quickly seek out deeper waters to find suitable prey.

Savage Sea-hunter. Whether feeding on sea life in the deepest ocean trenches or nesting in the shallows along the world's temperate coasts, the slaughtermaw lamprey is a fearsome predator that inspires fear and respect in seafarers and land-dwellers alike. While stories of megalodons, giant squid, and whales tend to be more prevalent, those who have encountered a slaughtermaw lamprey while at sea spin harrowing tales of survival against one of the harsh planet's most voracious hunters. Despite being jawless, a slaughtermaw lamprey's powerful bite can pierce through even the toughest of hides and sailors speak of a slaughtermaw lamprey's bite being capable of sinking waterborne craft as they tear through hulls seeking a meal. Slaughtermaw lampreys seem to fear no creature and many a sea creature has been seen sporting the ring-shaped scars left by their attacks. Fortunately, slaughtermaw lampreys are rare during most of the year, only coming into contact with humanoids during their mating season when they venture from the icy depths to shallower coastal regions. A slaughtermaw lamprey can grow to reach an impressive fifteen feet in length and typically weigh about nine hundred pounds. Slaughtermaw lampreys typically live ten to fifteen years, though older (and frighteningly, larger) members of their species are a part of many seafaring tales.

Deep Diver. A slaughtermaw lamprey spends much of its time feeding within the ocean trenches or along the ocean floor, attacking squids, sharks, and whales that swim by them. Typically, slaughtermaw lampreys prey upon whales, but they do attack larger predators such as megalodons and giant squids

alone. Rare occurrences of multiple slaughtermaw lampreys feeding and hunting together to bring down larger prey is the stuff of nightmares. While squids can easily fight back, whales and sharks have a harder time defending themselves against even a solitary slaughtermaw lamprey. Both whales and sharks will often rise to the surface quickly, which typically causes the lamprey to detach as the rapid pressure change causes them to become confused and disorientated.

Light-Eater. Slaughtermaw lampreys have a habit of seeking out anything that radiates bright light or warmth, which some species of predators have turned into an advantage, such as the notorious deeplight hungerer, which utilizes bright glowing lures to attract them in the darkness of the deepest trenches. Given enough time to adapt, they can rise to the surface to hunt, but it must be done slowly. While they focus on larger prey that can give them a larger meal, they have been known to attack smaller prey on occasion during their mating season, when they congregate along the shore and come into contact with humanoids and giants. Ships are particularly vulnerable as they resemble whales to slaughtermaw lampreys, and their teeth can easily puncture through armored hulls. As a ship begins to take on water, slaughtermaw lampreys will feast upon anything that tries to swim to safety, or in the case of larger ships swim inside the flooded cabins to snatch up stragglers.

Legendary Sea Monsters. A mixture of fear and reverence surrounds the slaughtermaw lamprey and some cultures have elaborate rituals around interacting with them. Some giant clan believe that within each lamprey is the soul of a powerful warrior who died outside of battle, destined to hunger for glory and bloodshed but never quite sating urges they no longer understand. Despite a rather gruesome coming-of-age ritual involving stealing lamprey eggs from a nest guarded by two mated lampreys, several more traditions exist to honor

the lampreys, including blood sacrifice and offerings of live food. Artifacts originating from hill and stone giants, such as scrimshawed whale bones and shells depicting great battles or attacks made by lampreys and other creatures, can be found across coastal regions where lampreys can be found.

SLAUGHTERMAW LAMPREY

Large beast, unaligned

Armor Class 16 (natural armour)

Hit Points 210 (20d10+100)

Speed 15 ft., swim 60 ft.

STR	DEX	CON	INT	WIS	CHA
23 (+6)	18 (+4)	20 (+5)	2 (-4)	16 (+3)	12 (+1)

Saving Throws Str +10, Con +9

Skills Athletics +10, Perception +7

Damage Immunities cold

Senses darkvision 60 ft., passive Perception 17

Languages -

Challenge 10 (5,900 XP)

Feed. The slaughtermaw lamprey is nourished by blood. Every time a slaughtermaw lamprey causes damage to a Medium or larger creature that has blood or an equivalent substance with a bite, it regains 27 (6d8) hit points.

Vanishingly Quick. The slaughtermaw lamprey is such a swift and agile swimmer that, whilst underwater, its movements do not provoke opportunity attacks.

ACTIONS

Multiattack. The slaughtermaw lamprey makes three attacks, two with its bite and one with its stinger slam.

Bite. *Melee Weapon Attack:* +10 to hit, reach 15 ft., one target. *Hit:* 28 (4d10 + 6) piercing damage. If the target is a creature, it must succeed on a DC 17 Constitution saving throw or have its hit point maximum reduced by an amount equal to the damage taken. The target dies if this attack reduces its hit point maximum to 0. The reduction lasts until removed by the *greater restoration* spell or other magic.

Stinger Slam. *Melee Weapon Attack.* +10 to hit, reach 10 ft., one target *Hit.* 17 (2d10 + 6) bludgeoning damage and the target must succeed on a DC 17 Constitution saving throw or be paralyzed for 3 (1d4+1) rounds. The target may repeat the saving throw at the end of each of its turns, on a success the condition ends.

Shattering Fangs. The slaughtermaw lamprey has a vicious bite of tough, razor-sharp teeth, fully capable of penetrating the thickest of hides or armors. If both the slaughtermaw lamprey's bites hit the same creature, the slaughtermaw lamprey may, as a bonus action, also apply the damage of the second bite to the target's armor or shield, if any. The armor takes a permanent and cumulative

-1 penalty to the AC it offers for every 10 points of damage the slaughtermaw lamprey's bite inflicts on it. Armor reduced to an AC of 10, or shields that drops to a +0 bonus, are destroyed. The creature no longer gains any benefit from the armor, but subject to GM's approval, the shredded remnants of magic armor or shields may be reforged by a master smith.

ALCHEMICAL USES OF A LAMPREY

Though exceptionally dangerous, some hunt the slaughtermaw lamprey to render its oil and capture its eggs, as both are highly prized by alchemists.

Dried Slaughtermaw Eggs: When raw slaughtermaw lamprey eggs are quickly dried and eaten, the toxins in the eggs cause the user to experience intense feelings of euphoria, coupled with feelings of greater strength and stamina than normal in oneself. However, this takes its toll on the user's mind, causing them to make progressively poorer decisions and can lead to periods of aggression or confusion with overuse. For 3 (1d6) hours after consumption the creature gains advantage on Charisma (Intimidation) checks, and if they possess the barbarian's Rage feature, they gain two extra uses of it while this effect of consuming dried slaughtermaw eggs persists.

However, for 6 (1d12) hours the creature is belligerent, constantly picking fights with other creatures, has poor impulse control, and has disadvantage on Wisdom (Perception) checks. With subsequent uses the danger of suffering a mental breakdown increase: Whenever a creature consumes more than one dose of dried slaughtermaw eggs per week, the creature must pass a DC 14 Charisma saving throw at the end of the period of poor impulse control or obtain a random long-term madness (as described in the **5E SRD**). For each use of this drug, the DC increases by a cumulative +1. This resets only if a user has not consumed dried slaughtermaw eggs for a whole month. **Price** 1,800 gp.

Slaughtermaw Oil: Refined from the fatty tissues of slaughtermaw lampreys, this oil is quite sticky and highly flammable, creating a noisome green fire when burned. Torches and lanterns can burn this alongside their normal fuel to double how long they last. Additionally, it can be combined with alchemist's fire to create a hotter and longer lasting fire. When slaughtermaw oil is added to a flask of alchemist's fire increase the fire damage of the alchemist fire by 2 (1d4) and increase the DC of the Dexterity check to extinguish the flames to 12. Additionally, alchemist's fire treated with slaughtermaw oil can be used underwater. **Price**: 5 gp.

SQUID, GIANT

Immense in size, this great squid's tentacles writhe and flash with almost nauseating speed. The beast's eyes are as big as shields. The giant squid is a legendary beast capable of feeding on humans with ease. Hunger has been known to drive these normally deep-dwelling creatures up to the ocean surface where anything they encounter is potential prey.

GIANT SQUID

Huge beast, unaligned

Armor Class 15 (natural armor)

Hit Points 133 (14d12+42)

Speed swim 60 ft.

STR	DEX	CON	INT	WIS	CHA
19 (+4)	15 (+2)	16 (+3)	2 (-4)	12 (+1)	2 (-4)

Skills Perception +4, Stealth +5

Senses darkvision 60 ft.; passive Perception 14

Languages —

Challenge 5 (1,800 XP)

Underwater Camouflage. The giant squid has advantage on Dexterity (Stealth) checks made while underwater.

Water Breathing. The giant squid can breathe only underwater.

ACTIONS

Multiattack. The giant squid makes two attacks: one with its bite and one with its arms. It may substitute a tentacle attack in place of a bite or arms, or both.

Bite. *Melee Weapon Attack:* +7 to hit, reach 5 ft., one target. *Hit:* 11 (2d6+4) piercing damage.

Arms. *Melee Weapon Attack:* +7 to hit, reach 15 ft., one target. *Hit:* 21 (4d6+7) bludgeoning damage.

Tentacle. *Melee Weapon Attack:* +7 to hit, reach 30 ft., one target. *Hit:* 13 (2d6+7) bludgeoning damage and the target is grappled (escape DC 17). Until this grapple ends, the creature is restrained. The giant squid has two tentacles, each of which can grapple one target.

Ink Cloud (Recharges after a Short or Long Rest). A 20-foot-radius cloud of ink extends all around the giant squid if it is underwater. The area is heavily obscured for 1 minute, although a significant current can disperse the ink. After releasing the ink, the giant squid can use the Jet action as a bonus action.

Jet. Until the end of its turn, the giant squid's swim speed is 240 feet if it moves in a relatively straight path.

TRITON

These aquatic beings resemble merfolk, except where a merman has a single fish tail, a triton has two scaly, finned legs. They are the watchers of the sea, often using dolphins or other aquatic creatures as mounts, and maintaining a vigil against the evil races below the waves. Their coloration ranges from silvery to aqua blue and kelp green to coral and salmon. Older tritons often have barnacles, corals, and seashells crusting the back, chest, and shoulders, worn almost like jewelry as a mark of status among their kind. Their hair and fin color usually matches their other coloration, but white hair is also common. Tritons' eyes shine like sunlight upon a clear sea. A typical triton stands 6 feet in height and weighs 180 pounds.

Peaceful Guardians. Tritons make their homes on the sea floor, growing coral reefs and sculpting stones into gentle arcs to create living spaces that are beautiful and natural-looking. Many of these sites lie near great thermal vents, providing not only heat but also rich minerals and nutrients for the fish and other creatures tritons eat. Tritons can breathe air or water but prefer water. While their cities are designed for water-breathers, they usually feature one or two airtight buildings set aside to hold air for landwalking visitors. Triton settlements can be found anywhere from arctic to tropical waters, but most are in temperate locations. They generally avoid the deepest reaches of the ocean, for it is here that creatures like aboleths and krakens rule—creatures that the tritons have long waged war against.

Elemental Origin. Originally hailing from the Plane of Water, long ago the triton race migrated to the oceans of the Material Plane, and they are now fully adapted to life there. Their split legs allow them to hobble about slowly on land, but they rarely do so, preferring their natural environment and the greater mobility their forms afford there.

TRITON

Medium humanoid, neutral good

Armor Class 14 (scale mail)

Hit Points 60 (11d8 + 11)

Speed 30 ft., swim 30 ft.

STR	DEX	CON	INT	WIS	CHA
14 (+2)	11 (+0)	12 (+1)	13 (+1)	13 (+1)	10 (+0)

Saving Throws Dexterity +4, Wisdom +5

Skills Animal Handling +4, Athletics +6, Perception +5

Damage Resistances cold

Senses darkvision 60 ft., passive Perception 15

Languages Aquan, Common, Primordial, Sylvan

Challenge 2 (450 XP)

Amphibious. The triton can breathe air and water.

Fearless. The triton has advantage on saving throws against fear.

Life Aquatic. The triton can communicate with beasts that breathe water as if they shared a language and adds twice its proficiency bonus (+4) on Charisma (Animal Handling) checks with aquatic beasts.

Summon Ally (1/Day). The triton can summon an aquatic beast with a challenge 1 or lower, two beasts with challenge 1/2 or lower, or four beasts with challenge 1/4 or lower. The summoned allies have maximum hit points and serve as if the triton had cast *conjure animals*.

Trident Master. A trident used by a triton deals one extra die of damage on a hit (included in the attack).

ACTIONS

Multiattack. The triton makes two attacks with its trident or its bow.

Trident. *Melee Weapon Attack:* +4 to hit, reach 5 ft., one target. *Hit:* 11 (2d8+2) piercing damage.

Bow. *Ranged Weapon Attack:* +2 to hit, range 80/320 ft. (10/40 ft. underwater), one target. *Hit:* 5 (1d8+1) piercing damage. If one of the triton's summoned allies is adjacent to the target, the triton has advantage on ranged attacks with its bow.

WHALE

This immense whale has an enormous, box-shaped head over a massive, toothy maw. Its rough white hide is laced with scars. Legendary in size and temper, great white whales are far more aggressive than their smaller kin, over 80 feet long and weighing over 60 tons.

GREAT WHITE WHALE

Gargantuan beast, unaligned

Armor Class 17 (natural armor)

Hit Points 279 (18d20+90)

Speed 0 ft., swim 40 ft.

STR	DEX	CON	INT	WIS	CHA
30 (+10)	6 (-2)	20 (+5)	10 (+0)	12 (+1)	8 (-1)

Saving Throws Str +16, Dex +4, Con +11, Wis +7, Cha +5

Skills Insight +7, Perception +7, Stealth +4

Senses blindsight 120 ft.; passive Perception 17

Languages Aquan

Challenge 17 (18,000 XP)

Echolocation. The whale can't use its blindsight while deafened.

Hold Breath. The whale can hold its breath for 90 minutes.

Keen Hearing. The whale has advantage on Wisdom (Perception) checks that rely on hearing.

Legendary Resistance (1/Day). If the whale fails a saving throw, it can choose to succeed instead.

Siege Monster. The whale deals double damage to objects and structures.

ACTIONS

Bite. *Melee Weapon Attack:* +16 to hit, reach 20 ft., one target. *Hit:* 31 (6d6 + 10) piercing damage. If the whale scores a critical hit, it rolls damage dice three times, instead of twice.

Tail Slap. *Melee Weapon Attack:* +16 to hit, reach 30 ft., one target. *Hit:* 20 (3d6 + 10) bludgeoning damage.

Smashing Breach. A great white whale can make a special attack against creatures on the surface of the water. At the end of its movement, it can occupy one or more creature's spaces. Any Huge or smaller creatures in the whale's space must succeed at a DC 24 Dexterity saving throw or take 28 (4d8+10) bludgeoning damage and be forced into the nearest square that is adjacent to the whale. This breach automatically attempts to capsize any boats caught wholly or partially in this area. If the whale fails to displace everything in its space, it is forced back to its previous unoccupied location, or if that is not possible, the nearest space it can fit.

LEGENDARY ACTIONS

The great white whale can take 3 legendary actions, choosing from the options below. Only one legendary action option can be used at a time and only at the end of another creature's turn. The whale regains spent legendary actions at the start of his turn.

Detect. The whale makes a Wisdom (Perception) check.

Tail Attack. The whale makes a tail slap.

Underwater Surge (Costs 2 Actions). The whale moves up to its swim speed without provoking opportunity attacks and uses Smashing Breach.

Mythos Monsters

Mythos Monsters brings over 40 eldritch abominations from the dark places beyond the stars to your 5E campaign, with beautiful artwork for every one! Unleash the mind-bending majesty of the Lovecraft mythos on an unsuspecting world, with mythos minions like the **deep ones, faceless stalkers**, and the hideous hybrid **blood of Yog-Sothoth** and inhuman horrors like **shantaks, gugs, nightgaunts**, and the **hounds of Tindalos**, or terrifying titans like **bholes, primal shoggoths**, and **flying polyps**. Their unfathomable plots are guided by monstrous masters like the **mi-go, elder things,** and **denizens of Leng**, or even two of the Great Old Ones themselves in dread **Cthulhu** and **Hastur the Unspeakable**. Plus, you'll find tools and templates to turn ordinary monsters into pseudonatural **xenoid** monstrosities, with options for epic variants! The stars are right to pick up this spectacular 74-page supplement for 5th Edition and **Make Your Game Legendary!**

www.makeyourgamelegendary.com

5E

SEA MONSTERS